Praise for THE BONE INVENTORY

"Rissa does a beautiful job painting a picture of her world and how it has become this dystopian society. There was so much mystery, intrigue, and surprises that I didn't see coming! It was thrilling to see all of the pieces start to come together in her story, and makes me even more excited for the conclusion of her series!"

~Amber Crook

"I devoured this sci-fi novel like an alien sucking up Earth's snacks! Initially, I tried piecing together how it'd link up with the others, considering they were extraterrestrial-free zones. Early on, I took some wild stabs, and by the finale, everything magically aligned. Those surprise

memories "Brad" dug up, especially Spencer-related ones, totally threw me. Marissa's writing is pure magic, folks!"
 ~MellissaMae

"This book is out of this world This book, just like Stars Like Acid (which is AMAZING) is something that I don't normally read. But I am so dang glad that I found them! I love the storyline, the characters that I can actually relate to, and the different look on this world. Marissa's writing style is unreal and I love getting lost in her worlds "
 ~Jessica Grooms

""We fight for the stars, and the stars for us."

I can always count on Marissa Lupe for three things: A diverse cast of characters, beautiful graphics printed on her pages, and an action-packed Sci-Fi story. Marissa and I have been instagram buddies for a while now, and I loved her debut novel, Stars Like Acid, so when she told me that The Bone Inventory was a prequel to the Stars Like Acid series, I signed up to be an ARC reader without hesitation!

Chapter one hooked me right away and left me wanting to know more. I love when a book drops you into action with just enough mystery to keep you turning the page. I ended up finishing the book in 3 days because I found myself thinking about it and wondering where it was all headed.
I also enjoyed that each chapter title was a song. When I

asked Marissa about it, she said the songs represent the mood of each chapter- sort of like a book soundtrack!

The Bone Inventory is described as having vibes similar to The Host by Stephanie Meyer and I couldn't agree more. If you like sci-fi stories with strong relationship storylines you will like The Bone Inventory. Check it out!"
~Nikki Blake

"Alien body snatcher romance. It's never quite that simple. When you can live forever, traipsing the galaxy with the no end goal hey would you stay on Earth? Unless you found the one you're meant to be with... but is it mutual? Will the others let you stray from your mission?
I loved this read so much. It's uniqueness was draws you in, and you have to know what happens next. The character personalities had me giggling consistently. Even if sci-fi isn't your norm, you should give it a read ;)"
~Amanda Miller

Also By Marissa Lupe

Book One:
STARS LIKE ACID
Book Two:
STARS LIKE FIRE
Prequel:
THE BONE INVENTORY

Stars Like Rain

Book Three of the Stars Like Acid series

Marissa Lupe

Howlite Publishing LLC

Howlite Publishing LLC
Meeker, CO
United States
marissalupe.com
Stars Like Rain

First Edition, 2025

eBook ISBN: 978-1-960824-09-7
Paperbook ISBN: 978-1-960824-10-3
Hardback ISBN: 978-1-960824-11-0
Library of Congress Control Number: 2025904315
Fiction/ScienceFiction/General

Formatting interior book design and cover art by
Howlite Publishing LLC

To those who are strong enough to admit when they are
wrong.
To those brave enough to grow.
To those who can spend hours staring at the stars.
To those who see the magic all around us.
and
To you dear reader... Thank you.

Contents

Twenty years later...

Chapter One

Every pounding footstep ground a deeper connection to the planet as she raced through the forest laughing. She was free. The deep purple soft and silky branches whipped through her hair and tickled her face. No one was here to tell her how reckless her behavior was, or implore her to be more careful. Here, in the wild, she could unburden herself from the restraints her community had put on her. She was no ruler, no leader.

She was just... Celia.

Carefree and at one with nature.

The Sanctuary had much better options for their next leader, so why choose her? Celia's powers were useless on this planet, her home Meraiis, the only place she had ever known. As far as the elders could tell, there was no longer poison seeping through the human pores. Her only appeal to the people was the fact that she was her daughter. She did not want Téa's legacy, she wanted to make her own path, lead her own future, explore the world. Why was that so hard for them to understand?

It was all her fault, for training Celia the way that she did, for raising her the way she did. It wasn't Celia's fault her mother prepared her to be a leader. She had fought back as much as she could. Stomped her feet before every lesson. Purposefully let her opponents win. No matter how hard she tried, her parents pressed on, insisting that someday she would be grateful for her skills.

Why couldn't Emma be her mom? Emma took care of her more than Téa anyway. Her cousins had it easy. All they had to do was go to school and have fun and grow up to be assigned whatever position within the Sanctuary they wanted. Being a royal family had its benefits for everyone except Celia. It was not fair.

Elijah would understand, she missed her brother dearly. As soon as he was of age he moved outside the Sanctuary walls, that was ten years ago. She was twenty now and still hadn't seen the world. She begged him all the time to move back to the Sanctuary. But his response was always the same, "It's too loud for me there."

Celia rolled her eyes at the memory. Too loud.

What a poor excuse to leave her behind.

Celia's laughter turned to anger as she ran forward, pushing herself faster and faster. Pumping her legs and moving her body to its limit. When she could take no more and her lungs burned from the effort she collapsed. Her blood pulsated in her ears as she sat crying on the forest floor. The loneliness enveloped her. Wrapped itself around her like a blanket. When her breathing slowed and feeling returned to her legs, she wiped at her watery eyes and gasped.

She was surrounded by red foliage.

When she looked behind her, she could see how the bright red gradually faded back into the deep purple. She was only a few yards outside the boundary, if she hurried back maybe she could make it in time. Her heart pounded as fear settled into place, completely replacing the sadness with anxiety.

Too late.

She looked up into the blackened eyes of a thick masculine elk. Its breath formed clouds as it huffed out air through its wide hairy nostrils. He kicked up his hoofs and reared back ready to charge. Her scream echoed out to no one and as Celia tried to move there was only silence. The world around her slowed as the Elk stole her air. Her lungs ached as her breath slowly got sucked into the giant animal before her.

This was it.

This was going to be her end, what an unnecessary death this would be. She wondered only for a moment if her mother would mourn her death. She knew without a shadow of a doubt that her father would. The heartbreak would consume Zephyr.

Celia had to fight. She could not do this to her dad, die this way without trying. Celia struggled to her feet, but just as soon as she took one shaky step forward, she fell. Celia kneeled on one knee trying to push herself back up. The invisible waves of force that the elk was throwing at her were powerful. She had also made the mistake of screaming, giving all her air to its lungs instead of hers. Fighting back was futile, she'd suffocate soon.

Just as the world around her was growing dim and the ache in her chest unbearable, a pair of strong arms wrapped around her, helping her to her feet and they ran. Celia could only assume the figure running next to her was a man. Their body was masculine and tall, but his face was covered by the dark hooded tunic he wore.

A powerful crashing sound followed them as they ran, and Celia spared a glance behind her. There was no longer the lone elk, a dozen deer were following in his wake, chasing after them.

Twigs snapped and leaves flew, the ground reverberated with their power. The Elk was close enough to nip at the end of Celia's sweater, its gnashing teeth reaching for her as they ran, and just as it was going to be close enough to stab her with its mighty antlers, Celia and the stranger reached the dark line of lavender, plum, and majestic violets.

Safe.

The elk and deer were stopped in their tracks, they stomped their hooves in frustration as though there was an impenetrable shield stopping them from moving forward. Celia and the stranger were safe from the red territory of the hooved animals, the scream stealers.

They kept running a few more yards into the safety of the dark forest until they could no longer see the vicious animals they left behind. Celia stopped to catch her breath. To refill her lungs with precious oxygen. She doubled over from the effort of running, and when she stood back up to thank the stranger, he was gone. Vanished, as though he never existed at all. Celia turned in circles looking all around, but there was nothing, nobody.

Maybe she had hallucinated him? Oxygen-deprived brains have visualized worse. But those arms around her body had felt so real, so powerful. Celia began to shake as the adrenaline faded. Her instincts were to go back home, to start walking in the direction of the Sanctuary. But she had come this far, and she was secure in the boundary lines, so she turned in the direction of Elijah's cabin. A hug from her brother was just the thing she needed.

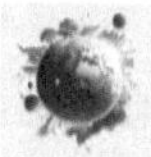

"Are you insane!?" Elijah paced his small living room, visibly shaking with anger. His wild curly red hair, taller than average height, and muscular build, only added to the intense energy of his words. "Coming all the way out here without an escort!? You could have been captured, injured, killed!"

Guilt was crawling all over Celia as she watched her brother panic. "Oh, come on Elijah, it's not so dangerous out there. You used to sneak out all the time!"

Her brother stopped and turned to face her. "That's different and you know it."

The injustice of it all boiled within her. Celia's anger was filling her up and she could no longer contain it. "Why!? Because I'm a woman!?"

Elijah dragged his hand down his face as an exasperated sigh escaped his lips. "No, Celia. It's because you're the future ruler of the Sanctuary." He took a deep breath and hesitated. "And those rumors about the indigenous, about what they do to women, that they would take you for their tribes without a second thought. Use every piece of you down to your bones. That's all bullshit. Just ignorant beliefs of racist people still stuck in the old ways. You don't have to fear them. But you do have to fear everything else that is out there. This planet is dangerous and unpredictable, and whether you like it or not, you're important to our people, Celia."

A chill crept up her spine and Celia chose to change the subject. She looked around the solid log cabin and her eyes landed on the elbow crutches hung on the wall. "Why do you keep those things? It's not like they're art."

Elijah stopped his pacing and stood next to Celia with his arms crossed. "I keep them as a reminder. To be grateful for the second chance we have been given and not to waste it." He glanced at her out of the corner of his eyes before saying. "You have no idea what it means to battle a serious illness. You know, I'm twenty-eight years old, and with my disease, if we were still on Earth, I could be dead by now. You'll never know what the flu is. You'll never have to see the ravages of cancer. You have no idea how lucky you are, Celia." He smiled at her. "This planet is dangerous, but it's also a gift, we need to respect and appreciate it."

She shuffled her feet and tried to shake off the dark and gloomy mood that seemed stuck to her like thick black goop.

Celia put her hands on her hips and mockingly shook a finger at him. "You know who's lucky? You are, because I'm cooking dinner!"

Celia flashed him a wide grin and skipped towards the kitchen. "I know you love my orange zest cinnamon rolls, how about breakfast for dinner?"

Elijah chuckled. "I know what you're trying to do. But I have to call mom and dad, they need to know you're here."

Celia let out a defeated sigh. "Ugh, just a few hours Elijah, please?" She clasped her hands together and took a pleading stance."

Elijah's face dropped. "I'm sorry Celia, I have to. But I'll try to negotiate dinner and me escorting you home. Deal?"

Celia grunted and plopped herself on the worn-out couch. "Fine." She waved a hand lazily in the air. "Do what you must."

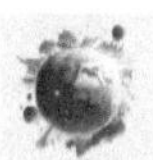

A handful of minutes later Elijah emerged from his radio room with a satisfied smirk on his face. "You are looking at the master." He said with a wink.

Hope jumped up in Celia's chest. "I get to stay for dinner?"

Elijah sat on the couch next to her. "Not only do you get to stay for dinner, but mom agreed, with some convincing from dad, that it would be better for me to escort you home in the morning, seeing as how it's so late and all."

Celia jumped up and danced frantically in excitement. "A whole night away from the Sanctuary? You are a miracle worker, big brother!" She clapped her hands together and smiled. "I'm making you the best cinnamon rolls you've ever had in your whole life!"

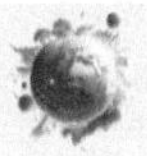

As the evening progressed and Celia worked the dough, a calm finally graced her tormented thoughts. If only for a night she would be able to breathe. To relax and not worry about the responsibilities that would soon be forced upon her.

With a quiet mind, she could not help but have her thoughts drift to the mysterious stranger who had saved her earlier. The more she thought about it, the more she was convinced that he was real. He saved her life and then ran away. Why?

Celia knew the repercussions of asking too many questions about their indigenous neighbors. But she was curious, and she knew just the person to ask. Her grandmother. Florence would be her first stop when she got back home, despite her mother's warning to stay away.

Chapter Two

As they walked back to the Sanctuary, Celia could see the weight of being nearby, hang heavy on Elijah's shoulders. According to her mother, every person who had abilities on Earth had their powers altered or amplified on Meraiis. Elijah, who could see and speak to the dead, could now also hear the thoughts of those around him. He had yet to figure out a way to control it, a way to turn the faucet of noise off.

He slowed his pace as they got nearer. "I hate it here, it's so loud, C."

Celia grimaced at his pain. "I'm sorry big brother. I wish mom would let me visit you more so you wouldn't be so alone all the time. I know how hard it is for you to come to the Sanctuary."

He graciously smiled for her even though she knew he was far from happy. "Me too little sis, me too."

She saw the hesitation etched all over his face as they walked and shook her head. "Go ahead, say it."

Elijah sighed deeply as though bracing himself for the onslaught of her anger he knew his words would manifest. "You know, mom is never going to give you your freedom if you can't control yourself. Why were you running out here alone in the first place? You know it isn't safe without a guard."

A warm breeze gusted through her hair, and she opened her arms to the sky with a smile tugging at her lips. She twirled around taking in her surroundings. "Because it's real out here Elijah." She gestured around them. "Just soak it all in, for only a moment." She said as they walked.

She looked up to the wide-open lavender sky above that seemed to wave and dance like an ocean on land. Then she pointed at the two-way geysers in between the ruby rock formations. It was warm water that would shoot from a hole in the top of a stone mouth, land in a glistening pool of crystal-clear water below, then be pushed back up to where it came from, all the while maintaining its tube-like structure. Like an ever-flowing ring of water. Celia talked about the multi-colored plumage of the Meraiis birds, they were a bright spot mixed in with the clouds of brown sparrows that came with them from Earth.

Celia laughed as she twirled. "How could you not want to be in this nature all the time. Not only that, but also because I deserve freedom, brother. I shouldn't have to earn it, I should be able to take it as I please. I deserve to live in this new world just like everyone else. Look at the beauty of this place and I've barely experienced it." Celia came to a stop and dropped her arms. "I'm lonely, Elijah. You know girls my age aren't really girls at all, they're women. With jobs and boyfriends, sometimes they've even started families. Then there's me. Living the life of a child, controlled by the whims of her paranoid mother."

Elijah raised his head to the sky and groaned. "You really think that about mom? Truly? You think she's controlling you-because what?...She gets off on owning you?" He shook his head and took a step towards her. "You have no idea the sacrifices that woman has made for you. And the way she raised you was for your own good-for the good of everyone."

Celia's eyes gleamed in frustration, narrowing her gaze to a glare, feet firmly planted, and arms crossed. "So, you're on her side now, huh?"

"I'm on no one's side, I-"

"I thought you were my friend, brother. But you're just like her. Fine, you keep a lion caged for too long, someday it'll bite its handler's arm off you know."

A small satisfaction crept up Celia's sides as she watched the face of her brother pale in shock.

He was quiet before saying. "You know, I think you can make it back on your own from here." She watched him stuff his hands in his pockets, his shoulders curve in on themselves, and as he walked past her, she just barely heard his whispered non-goodbye. "My head is killing me."

Only as she watched his back move further into the distance, did a slight amount of remorse take place. Maybe that was a little harsh. She shrugged it off, and when she turned to continue on her way she stopped and smiled at a little light blue ball of fur emerging from its rabbit hole.

"Hey there little guy, you have freedom don't you? I bet you don't have a rabbit mom controlling your every move." Celia moved slowly trying to soften her steps, and just as she was about to reach out for a stroke of soft fur, the small creature stilled. It lay down unmoving, and its fur darkened to a deeper shade of blue.

Curiosity knotted her brow together and she touched the rabbit. No breath moved through the rabbit, it's still form already losing its heat, and as she pet the tiny animal, she wondered, how could a living thing die so quickly.

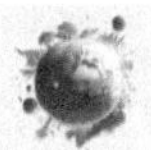

As Celia got closer to the Sanctuary, she could see the top of the clear open-air dome. The Sanctuary was like a city inside a giant clear egg. Layers of soil at the bottom, with manmade stairs leading from the Earth territory of Meraiis to the Sanctuary within the dome.

Moments later she stood in front of the grand stairs, the only way in or out. There were hundreds of massive ruby rock steps, each only two feet tall, but ten feet wide and five feet deep, like two grown men end to end, leading up to the entrance of the clear dome that surrounded the Sanctuary.

Twenty square miles of Earth were teleported here two decades ago, the last bit of Earth. The street level of the Sanctuary within the dome was a quarter mile high. The original founders spent years using ropes, ladders, and their abilities to build steps using the ruby rock from a nearby mountain.

Celia marveled at the drastic difference between the brown dull colors of Earth inside the dome, and the vibrant hues of the Earth territory of Meraiis surrounding it, as she climbed her way back to the Sanctuary.

Her breath came in sharp and ragged from the cool air, little puffs of mist clouded her view. Celia was fast reminded why a majority of the civilians never left the Sanctuary to explore the Earth territory of Meraiis surrounding the dome. Besides the treaty made with the indigenous peoples of Meraiis that kept the Earth survivors within close range of the Sanctuary, the climb alone was enough motivation to stay within the dome city. Her legs were beginning to burn with each step, her ribcage ached in protest from the effort of bringing air in and out of her lungs.

The city noise grew louder, and the savory scent of breakfast wafted towards her as she reached the midway point. As she continued her climb upwards Celia began to hear the activity of the Sanctuary above. People coming and going about the town, accomplishing their daily tasks. When she finally ascended to the street level, she was greeted by her mother's guard.

Celia's stomach dropped to her knees as she took that final step to the top and made eye contact with the massive man before her. "Hey, how's it going Brody? Been waiting long?" She let out a shaky chuckle hoping he was in a good mood today. And when she met his steely dark-eyed gaze and set jaw, Celia realized she would have no such luck.

Brody ran his fingers through his dark shoulder-length wavy hair, then crossed his solid arms. "Do you have any idea what you have put your mother through? She didn't sleep a wink all night!"

Celia rolled her eyes and started to walk past him. "Really? Sleep a wink? How old are you again? You talk like my great-grandmother."

Brody paused in disbelief, panic flooding his brown eyes. "You haven't been visiting Florence again, have you? You know it's not safe, even in death that old hag has a twisted sense of a moral compass."

Celia paused and turned to face him with her feet firmly planted. "So. What if I have? She's my great-grandmother Brody, she cares about me more than most living people."

The two began to walk again in silence, marinating on Celia's words. Brody broke the tension first. "What about me? I care about you, Celia. And your father, he's your soulmate for crying out loud. You really think no one cares about you?"

Celia turned on a heel, stopping again. "My mother sure doesn't! Keeping me locked up and isolated the way she has. She doesn't listen to me."

She knew then that she had gone too far, she could feel the frustration radiating off of him and he glared at her. His words came out like icicles. "I would hardly say you've been locked up, Celia. Maybe try being grateful for all that you have been given. At least you have a family."

She knew it was coming, he always played the orphan card. Being an orphan, Brody always had that line in his back pocket. But he wasn't wrong. She couldn't imagine having no one, not a single person with a blood relation to share your life with. He was only two years old when the mass extinction event occurred on planet Earth twenty years ago. After the teleportation to Meraiis, her mother had found him, barely able to walk on his little chubby legs, crying at the edge of the Sanctuary perimeter. No one in the Sanctuary claimed him. Téa guessed that his family was able to get him within the dome in time somehow, but not themselves.

Celia and Brody grew up together, along with her cousins. Guilt warmed her ears and she dropped her head, words coming out nearly a whisper. "I'm sorry, you're right. It's just hard sometimes, you know? The weight of responsibility." She paused and nudged his shoulder. "But you do have family Brody, you have me, my mom, my dad, even the cousins. We all claim you as our own, you know that."

He sighed deeply and shook his head. "And I'm grateful for that, but it's not the same and you know it." His cheeks blushed as he turned his gaze away. "I hardly think of you as a sister, Celia."

Celia gulped, tried to rub the tingling feeling away from her arms, and shuffled her feet. "Come on, let's keep going. The sooner I get this over with, the better."

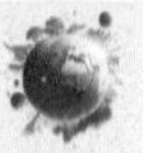

As they walked through the Sanctuary, Brody stood close enough to her that she could feel the heat coming off his body, hear his steady breathing.

She tried not to focus on him, and instead, to take in her surroundings and the various supernatural abilities of the locals. She never tired of watching peoples' power in action, and deep down, she had a mild jealousy, or perhaps sadness, that she lacked any actionable capabilities of her own.

The delectable sweet and yeasty smells coming from the bakery, made her mouth water; and the baker kneading the dough with his mind brought a smile to her lips. Children running through the colorful yet faded rock paved pathways, blew wind at each other to change their directions, like a heightened game of chase.

A carpenter used his super strength to carry a stack of ten tree logs, piled higher than two of himself. The original brown wood structures of the Sanctuary were mostly in need of repair. Their roofs were mixed with the newer, purple-colored houses built with the Meraiis wood from the surrounding forest. After twenty years the Sanctuary had become crowded, but it was all Celia knew.

The close quarters and over-filled houses were a familiar comfort. The community worked together to try and keep the last bit of Earth alive. But she heard the whisperings during her mother's meetings when Celia would hide around the corner to eavesdrop on private conversations. The Sanctuary was overwhelmed.

Before long the community would have to adapt to the land of Meraiis outside the dome. But the treaty was clear. They could not expand beyond the territory line, a mere five square miles outside the dome shell. Elijah was the only Earthling living outside the dome, just on the edge of the treaty line. Even if they expanded, it wouldn't last long before that space too would be overpopulated. The only solution would eventually have to be acceptance by the indigenous of Meraiis.

Anger started to rise within Celia again. What would her mother be leaving her with? These would be problems that would fall onto Celia's shoulders. She never asked for this, to be a leader someday. To be the one people relied on for answers. She did not ask to be Earth's savior. Hadn't she done enough just by being born? She had already given planet Earth a second chance, it wasn't her fault it got knocked out by a meteorite. When would she get to make her own choices? To live for herself.

A trill whistle from above snagged her ears, drawing her from the deep reverie of thought, signaling her arrival. The grand house before them was built entirely from Meraiis materials. Bigger than any other home, presumably made so spacious as to accommodate her parent's staff and offices. But all Celia saw was ostentatious greed, when all the other residents lived in such tight quarters with one another.

Celia took a deep breath and begrudgingly walked the five stone steps up to the double-wide ornately carved, soft lavender wooden doors. Before she could pull one open it swung out swiftly in front of her. Her mother, just as graceful and beautiful as ever, hurried out and wrapped her arms tightly around Celia. She could feel her mother's body shake with sobs of relief, and for just a moment, she regretted ever doubting her mother's love.

Chapter Three

As her mother's crying steadied into calm breathing, Celia knew the repercussions of her actions would be coming next.

Téa's slow breaths turned to frustrations that were palpable. "Celia, what on Earth were you thinking!?"

Celia laughed sarcastically. "We're not on planet Earth anymore, mother, or have you forgotten."

Celia instantly regretted talking back the second the words left her mouth.

Shut up, Celia.

The flare in her mother's nostrils, and flash in her eyes, told Celia what was coming next.

"Don't. Don't you dare be smart with me. Not now, not ever."

Celia knew she should keep her mouth shut, yet the rebuttal tumbled from her mouth regardless. "I'm not a child anymore, mother. I should be able to come and go as I please without causing a storm of panic!"

Seeing her mother's patience and unnerved stoic stance was more terrifying than any shouting match could ever be. Celia curled into herself preparing for the verbal onslaught that surely was to come. But when Téa wordlessly turned and walked away, Celia was left feeling unsteady.

She could hear her mother's voice from a few feet ahead. "Come, dinner is nearly ready, your father is waiting."

Celia reluctantly followed her mother's lead, Brody walking a step behind her. He whispered in her ear. "You just can't help yourself, can you?"

He chuckled next to her and she shot him a terse glare that snapped his jaw shut. Remorse crept up her belly as she watched him shake his head and split off from her and her mother.

Walking in silence Celia could not understand the turmoil within herself. She had a good life. Two loving parents, a brother that supported her, cousins, aunts, uncles. She was surrounded by a loving family. But that nagging little voice in the back of her head would never quiet. Incessant with its poisonous words flooding her mind with the hypocrisies of life.

Celia may have familial support, yet she was also bound by duty and responsibility by those same people. She had food, clean water, and a roof over her head. Yet she was still villainized by some Sanctuary civilians for her privilege.

The sharp claws of insecurity wormed their way through her thoughts and dragged her down into an abyss of depression. She could not see the light of the world, so consumed as she was by the darkness.

But then there would be a moment of fresh air, and her joy would return. She could see the beauty and color of life again. The clarity was stronger away from the Sanctuary. Leaving the Sanctuary was the only way she could hold onto her peace. She must make her parents understand. This was her life, and she should be free to make her own choices, duty-bound or not.

As they entered the dining hall, the tight coil of anxiety eased away from her chest. Zephyr hurried to her from across the room. Her father's wide-open embrace and ear-to-ear grin warmed her heart. How could I ever leave him?

Held tight in her father's arms, Celia couldn't remember why she would want to leave so badly. She loved it here. With their library of donated books from Sanctuary members, and warm rooms that chased away the darkness. At home in her bubble of comfort, she was content. She only needed them to understand that the weight of ruling the Sanctuary someday was too much.

She allowed the pure love from her father to flood through her, staunching the ebb of unpleasant thoughts. The way he always smelled of fresh cedar and lilacs. The way his sparse strands of gray hair intermingled in his thick head of dark blonde hair, and matched his shining gray eyes the same as her own. The way his light beard tickled her cheek when he brought her in for his bear hugs. Here she was safe, here she was home.

His voice was warm, familiar. "Hey kiddo, I missed you."

"I missed you too, dad."

The warmth of his hug melted away as he released her. "Your mother and I were both so worried, why did you run off like that? We searched the entire Sanctuary, why would you leave the dome?"

Celia tugged on her sleeve ends and shuffled her feet. "I'm not sure. Taking that tour yesterday to meet with the heads of all the different departments, just got to be too much. I had to get out."

She could feel the unease start to build within her father from their soulmate connection. He's worried about me, why is he so worried?

She slowly took her seat at the table and cleared her throat. Her pulse quickened and she clenched her hands, but she had to get the words out. "Mom, Dad, I don't think I have it in me to be leader of the Sanctuary. It's not what I want from my life."

Silence fermented around them, the toxic buildup from the absence of words overwhelmed her.

Until finally, her mother spoke. "Celia, I wish it were that easy. I only desire your happiness, but unfortunately, we don't have that luxury. I'm sure you're aware, but our community will soon outgrow the Sanctuary borders. Before long we will have to revise our treaty with the people of Meraiis and when that time comes, they will expect my direct descendant to take my place."

Celia could feel the tension coming off her father as her mother took a breath and continued to speak. "They honor family above all else, and if I do not appoint my direct heir as the future ruler of the Sanctuary, they will see me pushing you aside as dishonorable. They will view our entire civilization as untrustworthy, and negotiations would cease to be. Without more land, our people will die."

Celia dropped her head and stared at her hands in her lap. The unfairness of it all, gave fuel to the despair within her. Her words coming out in barely a whisper. "What about Elijah, he's your son too you know."

Her mother sighed deeply and gave a small shake of her head. "Of course he's my son, but you are well aware that they don't trust him. They met him just the one time shortly after our arrival, and his ability to read thoughts frightened them. Even though the Meraiis people communicate telepathically, that's different from someone being able to read another's inner-most thoughts. They hardly allow his presence so close to their borders, let alone for him to actually be Sanctuary leader."

She watched her mother leave her chair and make her way over to where Celia sat. She could feel the warm caress of her mother's hand on her back as she whispered. "I'm sorry my darling. But please try to see the good in this situation. You have a kind heart, you can ensure our people continue to grow and thrive. It's an opportunity for good, not the shackles you feel they are."

Celia could only nod, and her mother went back to her place at the head of the table. The remainder of dinner was quiet. She could scarcely hear the pleasantries of her parent's conversation as her own thoughts drowned out any other sound.

There must be another way. There had to be a better solution. She only had to make it through dinner, then she could sneak away to visit Florence. Her great-grandmother would know what to do.

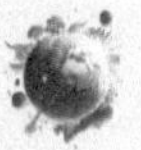

Only the faint pink hue from the multiple moons, streamed through the occasional window, guiding her way down the darkened hallway. Celia carefully tiptoed her way past her parents' partially opened bedroom door. She paused when she heard their quiet voices on the other side.

"Something is wrong, Téa, I can feel it. It's been building for a while, our girl is hurting."

"I would never want her to be in pain, you know that, Zephyr. But what can we do? I know this isn't what she wants, but turning down what is essentially a job, at the expense of thousands of people? And running away during an important meeting with heads of delegation, because she didn't want to be there?"

"Our duty is to our daughter Téa, and I'm telling you something is wrong. It's more than not wanting to be leader someday, it's something… deeper. I just can't seem to place what it is."

"She needs to grow up, Zephyr. She cannot behave like a child forever. This is her duty, her assignment, we all must play a role to keep our society thriving, and this is hers."

"I can't believe you would put duty above the emotional well-being of our daughter."

"That's not what I'm saying-"

Celia's heart dropped at the sounds of her parent's disagreeing voices, and it was her fault, they were arguing about her. She knew she was overreacting, it wasn't like her to run away from responsibility. But she could not deny the wrongness she was feeling within the Sanctuary walls. The off-kilter sensation had only grown ever since she had gotten more involved in the day-to-day tasks. Following her mother as Téa problem solved and negotiated with upset citizens was making her stomach turn.

She missed the quiet comfort of her books. The carefree joyfulness of her cousins, and Brody. They used to be all the social interaction she needed or wanted. Now she was meeting new people, shaking hands, and plastering on fake smiles. She didn't belong here. She only ever felt free outside of the dome. What kind of life would she live locked away by duty to her people?

Celia hesitated only a moment longer, before deciding she had to speak with her Great-Grandmother. She continued inch by inch through the mansion until she reached the front door; grateful that they only ever had one guard at night and he was reliably fast asleep. There was rarely violent unrest within the community, coupled with the fact that her mother and father had the strongest superpowers within the Sanctuary, there was not much need for security.

She carefully turned the handle of the front door, praying its squeaky hinges would not wake the guard. Slowly she slipped through the door and shut it behind her.

Outside the house, Celia took a deep breath of fresh air, smiling with the freedom the outdoors provided her. She loved the nights when most people were sleeping.

No small chat.

No random people commenting on the weather or asking if she had a 'special someone' yet. Out here, in the cover of night, she could be herself.

The dying leaves of birch trees crunched underfoot as she walked with her thoughts towards the fishpond. Celia could not remember what the fish looked like. Their water source dried out many years ago, and when the Sanctuary tried to integrate them into the water of Meraiis, the fish slowly died. While the people, livestock, deer, birds, and other animals from Earth acclimated well to their new water source, the fish did not.

The empty fishpond was within a small semi-sphere mud hut, and not large enough to build a home. So instead of tearing it down, the people of the Sanctuary agreed to transform it into a memorial site. Citizens could come and go to meditate or pray, or if they were lucky enough, even talk with family-linked souls who had made the journey to Meraiis with them, like her Great-Grandmother.

As Celia approached the entrance to the memorial site, she heard scuttling to her left. The night was quiet and a chill crept up her spine. She turned to look in the direction of the noise but could not see the source.

She called out. "Hello?"

Silence answered her call and little bumps of flesh dotted her skin. She rubbed her arms for warmth and to shake off the tension. Celia entered the semi-sphere. It took a moment for her eyes to adjust to the darkness pressing in on her. She carefully dug in her pocket and pulled out a candle and a matchbook that she had taken from her mother's emergency stash of supplies.

She carefully tore off one of the few remaining matches and struck it against the rough bottom of the matchbook, igniting a tiny flame that danced in the dark. Celia carefully lit the small half-used white candle and the memorial room was illuminated with the tiny yet powerful glow.

She walked into the empty pond and carefully sat crossed-legged on the smooth stone floor. Celia closed her eyes in concentration, trying to form the image of Florence's aged face.

Celia whispered into the quiet. "Grandmother, are you there?"

The noiseless echo of departed souls that she could not see, circled her. Even though she could not see or hear souls outside of her family tree, unlike Elijah, she knew they were there, circling like a school of hungry sharks, eager to connect to anyone in the living realm. The novelty of being able to see their loved ones after death eventually faded for the people of Earth. And just as the young generation had a tendency to forget their elders, leaving them to die slowly and alone, so too did the souls who had not moved on begin to be forgotten.

Celia called out to the darkness again. "Grandmother?"

She was beginning to lose hope. She wondered if, after all these years, Florence had finally found herself at peace and moved on. Celia picked up a small pebble next to her shoe and rolled it around between her fingers. The round coolness of it was a comforting distraction to her heavy thoughts.

Celia's hope deflated and she slowly began to stand, when a shout echoed across the spherical room, piercing the silence.

"Well hello my favorite Great-Granddaughter! To what do I owe the honor of your visit?"

Celia fell back on her bottom, her heart racing, and she grabbed at her chest. "Geez grandma, are you trying to give me a heart attack?"

Florence's ghostly form sat next to her, laughing and slapping her transparent knee. "Hey, give an old lady a break. I don't get much company these days, I have to find my entertainment somehow." The old woman continued to laugh, wiping away an imaginary tear, no doubt a habit from being alive longer than being dead.

Celia's breathing slowed and she shifted to find a more comfortable position, stretching her legs out in front of her and crossing them at the ankle, then leaned back on her elbows. "I need your help grandmother."

The old woman scoffed. "Ugh, don't call me that, it sounds so matronly, call me Florence darling."

Celia rolled her eyes. "Oh come on, don't be so dramatic, grandmother."

Florence steeled her gaze, mouth set. "It's Florence, dear. Now, why are you here."

Celia tried to shrug off the uncomfortable silence, sat back up, and crisscrossed her legs. She positioned herself with her back straight, head high, and hands in her lap. An attempt to feel more sure of herself at this moment than she really was.

"My mother wants me to become the next Sanctuary leader. But I don't want the position. It doesn't feel right in here, in the dome. I want to explore this world outside the confines that have been set for me. You knew her, before. When she was my age and just an ordinary girl. How can I get her to see that taking over for her is not what I want?"

Florence was quiet longer than Celia was prepared for. She started to wonder if Florence would be on her mother's side. If perhaps she was being childish at not accepting the role assigned to her. She shifted in her seat and resisted the urge to pick at her fingernails.

Finally, Florence responded. "Your mother will never concede. She's a fighter that one, and if her mind is made up then she will get what she wants. Perhaps you can approach the problem from a different angle, meet her halfway."

Celia tilted her head and looked at her grandmother. "What do you mean?"

"Well, I have been watching the happenings from my side, and I understand the people from Earth are outgrowing this small piece of the planet. Soon, you'll have to expand beyond the treaty lines. Maybe you can pitch Téa a new idea. You could be the liaison for Earth. Live near the boundary line with your brother and be the go-between for the people of Meraiis and the Sanctuary. It's not complete freedom, but it's a way for you to get outside of the Sanctuary, and still perform your civic duty to your people. One of your cousins can be a leader within the dome someday."

Celia's heart raced at the thought. Being a liaison would open so many doors for her, maybe the people of Meraiis would even let her travel their land someday. It could be a solution to all of her problems. But would her parents let her live outside the safety of the Sanctuary? She had to try. Her hope began to blossom again. She had a plan.

She turned to thank her great-grandmother, but Florence had already gone. Celia eased herself to a stance and blew out the candle. Enveloped in darkness once again, she made her way back home, and a smile lit her up from the inside.

I can do this, I can convince them to let me go.

Hope was a powerful thing, and with the joy warming her heart, Celia did not notice the darkness following her home.

CHAPTER FOUR

Celia was seated at the breakfast table with her parents. Her fruit oatmeal growing cold and the expression on her parent's faces dumbfounded. She had just dropped the informational bomb by voicing her request to be a liaison for the people from Earth. The silence from her parents permeated the room and produced a coldness in her chest, despite the crackling fire in the hearth that warmed her cheeks.

After what felt like an eternity, her mother cleared her throat. "Well, it seems as though you've given this a good deal of thought." She straightened the napkin in her lap and continued. "While I'm not completely comfortable with you living outside the dome, I do trust you to make good choices." She placed her elbows on the table and interlocked her fingers. "And despite what you may think, I do also wish for your happiness, sweetheart. So, if your father agrees, I am willing to give it a chance, on a trial basis of course."

Excitement drummed inside of Celia while she turned to look at her father with hopeful eyes. But through her connection, she could feel the hesitation coming from him. Zephyr slowly pushed his chair back and stood up. "I don't agree with this. I'm sorry Celia, but I can't agree with your mother on this one."

As her father walked away, it was as though an emotional slap reverberated across her face. She turned to look at her mother. Téa's jaw was dropped, it took a lot to shock her mother. Celia watched as Téa stood to follow after Zephyr. She paused to pat Celia's back. "Don't worry, I'll talk to him."

She watched her parents leave the room. Out of the hundreds of different ways she imagined this conversation ending, she never could have guessed her father to be the one holding her back from her freedom. Numbness traveled up from her toes and throughout her body, sitting still for long enough that her legs began to tingle. Finally, after the fire had died down to glowing embers, Celia left the dining table and headed outside to the stables.

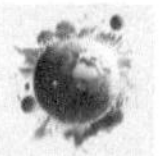

Celia found comfort in going through the tasks of caring for the horses. The calming motions of the brush gloved in her hand, stroking their manes and watching the twitching

waves of their skin as they nuzzled against her in appreciation, all brought a smile to her face. The scent of hay and
the sound of scooping cupfuls of grain into their feeders
was dependable. Even mucking the stalls had a familiarity
that eased her troubled thoughts.

She was feeding the last horse a special treat, her palm
flat as the equine beauty wiggled her whiskered lips across
the ruby red apple and gently picked the fruit up with its
teeth. Millie Mae, her favorite horse, crunched the apple
in delight. Celia lay her head into the thick of the horse's
neck, listening to it chew, and taking deep healing lungsful
of air. The neighing jealousy of the other horses brought
forth laughter from deep within Celia, and at last, she was
herself again.

Celia ran her hand across Millie Mae as the horse ate,
and she heard footsteps coming from behind her. Celia's
stomach dropped, but when her mother spoke, it had a hint
of a smile in it. "I thought I might find you here."

Celia dared not to let herself feel hopeful again, but it was
hard to deny when she turned and saw the joy on Téa's face.

"Your father has agreed to the trial basis, granted that
you have adequate protection. Congratulations, you are the
Sanctuary's new liaison."

Celia, an inch taller than her mother, with happy shock
racing through her body, ran into Téa's arms. "Thank you,
thank you, thank you!"

Her mother hugged her back. But her smile didn't reach
her eyes. Celia remembered the way she had been treating
her mother the past couple of days. Suddenly ashamed of

herself, she dropped her arms from the hug and shuffled her feet, clasping her hands together.

She tried to speak but the words got caught. She tried again. "Mom, I'm sorry for the way I've been behaving, and I'm sorry I ran out during the meetings."

Téa gestured to a small bench in front of the barn, and Celia took a seat next to her.

Celia took a deep breath and said. "I haven't felt myself lately, and when we were in that room with all those people talking about all their problems, I felt like I was suffocating. I couldn't take it anymore and I just started running, and didn't stop until I got to Elijah's."

She left out the part about crossing the boundary line. The guilt of lying by omission reared its ugly head, but Celia pushed the feeling down. Her mother did not need to know about her close encounter with the deer, or the mysterious stranger who had saved her. Not when she finally had a chance at a life outside the dome.

The silence from her mother was unsettling, but Celia kept herself patient. After a moment, Téa patted her leg and spoke without looking at her. "You and I have always told each other everything. But lately, I feel like I'm losing you. I responded out of fear yesterday, and I'm sorry too. I just want you to know that you can talk to me."

Celia dropped her head onto her mother's shoulders and held her mother's hand. "I know dad and I have our unique connection, but it's so easy with him, it's almost not real sometimes. More robotic being in each other's head. With you, it's different. I can talk to you and get my words out without you knowing exactly what I'm going to say ahead of time. I can express myself, and you never judge me." Celia took a deep breath of cool air and shuddered. "You're my best friend mom."

Her mother wrapped an arm around her and kissed the top of her head. They sat in the warmth of each other and Celia watched Téa wipe a tear from her eye. Celia may have her father's gray eyes, but she had her mother's features. She could see herself in her mother's features as they turned to look at each other. Her dark curly hair and gentle oval-shaped face.

Her mother's voice had the familiar gentleness she was used to when she spoke. "Whatever you're feeling, whatever you're going through, know that I'm here. You can talk to me anytime, and we can try and figure it out together."

Celia leaned against her mom again, breathing in the fresh cedar scent mixed with rose that seemed to only belong to her, and whispered. "Thanks, mom."

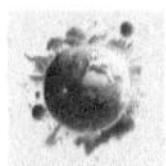

As they walked side by side back towards home, Celia's thoughts returned to her father's reaction this morning. "Hey, mom?"

"Mm-hmm?"

"Why didn't dad agree right away? I felt his hesitation, but he took off so fast, I couldn't feel what he was thinking beyond that."

Téa wrung her hands and glanced at her sideways before responding. "Your father was advocating for your happiness last night. We got into... a bit of a disagreement. But he wasn't anticipating you wanting to live outside the dome. He just thought you'd take a different position within the Sanctuary. I think maybe he was just scared for you, the thought of you being so far away."

Celia laughed. "It's only a handful of miles."

Téa grinned. "Yes, but you've been just down the hall your whole life. He worries for you, we both do. But you're right, it's time you had a life of your own, and we aren't going to stand in the way of that. Your father agrees."

Celia's joy was blossoming again, but one look from her mother brought back a small seed of doubt. "What? What is it?"

Téa cleared her throat, then looked at her and spoke. "Well, your father has agreed to let you live with Elijah, but given how reclusive your brother is, he's not exactly combat-trained. Your dad wants, Brody to go with you."

Celia came to a sudden stop and stared, mouth agape at her mother. "You can't be serious? He's not comfortable with me moving out of the home, but he's comfortable enough to let me live with Brody?"

Her mother's shoulders started to shake before the laughter came out in gasping intervals. When she calmed enough to talk, she playfully grabbed Celia by the shoulders. "Hey, you're the one who is supposed to understand your father. Don't ask me how his mind works. But it's not so bad, right? You and Brody are friends."

Celia dug a toe into the dirt. "Well yeah, but it's… weird."

Her mom wrapped an arm around her waist, and they continued on their walk. "You'll be okay, he's a good guy, Celia. And I can't say it's not comforting for me too, knowing you have a guard by your side."

Celia squinted her eyes. "Guard in training."

"Yes, well regardless, this is all good news, right?"

Celia's mouth tilted into a small smile, knowing that she was going to be living outside the dome. "Yeah, it's good."

Celia listened as the wind whistled through the treetops. The singing branches swayed as though the trees were passing secrets known only to them. She would miss the brown and green colored plant life of Earth, but it was not as though it was goodbye forever. As Celia and her mother got closer to home, she spotted her father waiting for them by the front door.

Téa patted her shoulder. "I'll see you both inside." She went through the front doors.

Celia stood, arms wrapped around herself and head down, she hated upsetting her father. She could count on one hand the times she had disappointed him, but she did not want to leave things on bad terms with him. Celia didn't know where to start and while she was searching for the right words, she was surprised when he spoke first.

"I'm sorry for being so short this morning, Celia."

She snapped her head up in surprise, not expecting the emotional waves of remorse coming from her father. She was so sure this morning that he was angry with her. Celia's mouth bobbed open and closed before pulling herself together and responding. "I thought you'd be mad at me."

He shook his head. "No, not at all." He sat on the front stone steps and patted the spot next to him.

Celia sat next to her father and waited for him to explain himself. He cleared his throat. "I know you're not a kid anymore. You've grown to be a smart, capable, and caring young woman. But you'll always be my little girl." He paused to give her a slight smile. "No parent ever wants their child to feel unsupported. They would never want their child thinking that they are incapable. A parent only wants them to feel loved and supported. And this morning, I feared I would fail you in this. Our connection is mostly a parenting benefit. As a baby and a toddler, I knew exactly what you were feeling, what you wanted, and how to care for you."

She watched her father shift uncomfortably in his seat, watched the fine lines in his hands twitch as he wrung them together. She tried to sense what he was feeling, but it was like trying to navigate through a fog, he was blocking her. She wondered why, but instead of asking she waited patiently for him to explain whatever it was, that he was trying to tell her.

He looked her in the eyes and spoke. "Do you remember when you were thirteen, and you talked back to your mother using your first swear word? You didn't realize right away that what you had done was so disrespectful because you were sensing my laughter."

"Yeah, I remember." She wasn't sure what point her father was trying to make but continued to listen.

"Sometimes, when you take me by surprise like that, my reactions are not the full truth, and not what I'd like you to think I believe. Of course I didn't think it was funny for you to call your mom that word. But, it took me by surprise, and when that happens it's more difficult for me to block our connection. I'm sure you know the amount of effort it takes."

She smiled at another memory. "Like when Brody and I thought it would be funny to sneak around in the middle of the night and take all the doors off the hinges, but you knew right away that I was guilty?" Her smile dropped, and she crinkled her forehead in thought. "Yeah, I know dad, I've never been able to block you like you've been able to block me on occasion. I know how difficult it is, what are you trying to say?"

"I had to walk away this morning because I had a lot of different emotions that I didn't want you to sense at that moment. You took me by surprise. But the only thing I ever want you to feel from me is love and support."

Celia laughed. "Well, that's a generalized impossibility father, but I suppose I understand what you're trying to say."

"Really, father." He gave her one of those, don't be a smartass kind of looks, before taking a deep breath. "What I'm trying to say is, I support you. Perhaps a change like this is exactly what you need."

Celia was perplexed. She knew she had been a little off yesterday, maybe more emotional than usual. But she knew he was holding back, hiding something from her. She was also relieved he did not seem mad at her and decided to take the win. "Well, thank you for your blessing, dad. I'll try not to disappoint you."

He pulled her into a side hug. "You are never a disappointment to me kiddo."

Celia drew comfort from the reconciliation with her parents and reveled in the new beginnings to come. Just as her excitement was about to kick into high gear, she noticed the fog had cleared from her father, and for just a moment she sensed fear. He stood and walked inside first, pausing and turning to see if Celia was following, and both shared wide smiles. His grin was genuine, hers was forced. He was unaware that he had let his guard down, but there was no mistaking it. Her father was not scared for her, he was scared of her.

Chapter Five

Celia's heart drummed against her chest, her excitement increased with every step towards freedom. She had spent all night getting ready, unable to sleep, too anxious to begin this next phase of her life. Now, as she walked the halls of her home, arms laden with bags, she had a minor sense of nostalgia.

She would miss this house, but now was not the time for tearful goodbyes. Now was the time to show them all how strong and capable she was for this assignment. She did not want a single doubt to plague her parents. Granted, her father was uncharacteristically distant all morning. Her leaving must be harder on him than she realized.

She had shaken off her odd encounter with him yesterday, she must have misread him. Why would he be scared of her? It had to have been a mistake. Pushing her concerns for her father aside she hurried through the front corridor, coming to a stop in the foyer.

Téa, Zephyr, Brody, and a couple of the manor employees were waiting for her. Celia beamed her happiness at them all and went to stand next to Brody.

Téa spoke to them both. "I trust you have everything you need?" They nodded in unison, and she continued. "If not, we're always here for you. It's not as though you are too far away. Please check in with me daily using the radio transceiver. Elijah said that it should not be a problem, don't make your mother worry, okay?"

Brody stepped forward to give her a hug. "Thanks for everything, Mrs. Garcia. I appreciate you trusting me with guarding your daughter. We'll check-in, I promise."

Téa cleared her throat and moved to stand in front of Celia. "Now, you understand how the locals work?" She didn't wait for a reply, Celia had been taught the customs from a young age. "We don't contact them, they contact us. You wait at the borderline, near the security outpost, and wait. Their sentries should spot you and make contact when they're ready."

Celia watched as her mother wrung her hands and her father leaned against the corner trying to block their connection. The most she could feel coming off of him was worry. Celia peeled her eyes away from him and focused again on her mother as she continued to speak.

"You have your soulmate connection with your father, so you're used to feeling another humans emotions. But, you've never had your mind invaded telepathically. It's difficult to get used to at first. It's strong, like a powerful tidal wave in your head. But you cannot show weakness or fear, be prepared. They will see any lie, so be honest.

Mentally, voice swiftly what your intentions are and what it is you seek, which is an allied relationship between our two nations. Then quiet your mind and wait for their answer. Do not argue with them if you don't get the answer you want. Report back to me after you've made first contact."

For the first time, doubt started to creep into Celia. She had not fully thought through what would happen next after getting her parents to agree. She was so excited about living on her own, she had forgotten that there was real and important work that came along with that freedom. The entire survival of the Sanctuary rested on her shoulders. It was up to her alone to negotiate a peaceful relationship with the people of Meraiis.

Her voice came out shakily. "I wonder if maybe you should be the one to make the first round of negotiations, mother?"

Téa smiled warmly and placed her hands on Celia's shoulders. "They only speak to one of us at a time. And if you want to be the liaison, you need to be the one to build that trust with them. Don't worry too much. It took several meetings before they agreed to our initial terms. Also, they are an honorable people, even if they don't agree, or if you accidentally offend them, they will not take back the land they have already given us. The Sanctuary still has five square miles outside of the dome that we can grow into. We have time."

Her mother's reassurance calmed Celia's beating heart. But she could still feel the small amounts of doubt and worry coming from her father. She looked to him. "Dad? What do you think?"

He pushed off the wall where he was leaning and went to her, he grasped her hands kindly. "My daughter, if anyone can pull this off, it's you. Don't forget, this was your idea, you have the passion for it, so I believe it will work out. You can bring peaceful negotiations between our two nations."

He dropped her hands and took a step back, crossing his arms and smiling. Celia wanted to believe him, but technically, this wasn't her idea, it was Florence's. All Celia wanted was a life of her own, freedom. Not this giant responsibility. But she could not tell them that, not now.

She plastered a smile on her face and tried to appear more confident than she truly felt. "Thanks, mom and dad, we'll check in regularly, promise."

Coldness snaked its way through her as she gave her final hugs goodbye and closed the door behind her with a loud click. She took a deep breath of fresh air, the wind whistled through the trees. She had not known that her hands were shaking until Brody gently pulled them into his own. He looked into her eyes, his voice deep and sure. "You okay?"

Were his lips always that smooth?

She shook her head and pulled her hands away from his. "Yeah, I'm good, thanks, Brody." She shot him a wide smile. "Are you ready?" And started walking without waiting for an answer. She heard his heavy footfalls hurrying to catch up, then his gruff reply. "Guess I'll have to be."

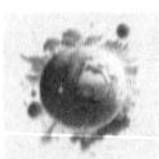

The hike down the dome took up a good part of the morning, the two blue flame suns were high in the sky by the time they were on their way to Elijah's.

Brody was oddly quiet so far, and she wondered if he was still mad at her for being in a shitty mood the other day. But then that thought brought an itch of irritation to her skin. Why should she have to be pleasant and agreeable all the time?

It was not like her to be so irritable in her thoughts. She tried to brush it off and bring forth her caring nature. She nudged his shoulder. "You're awfully quiet, what's up?"

He stopped in his tracks and stared at her incredulously. "Really, Celia? What's up?" He started pacing as his voice rose an octave. "Did you even once think about how I might be feeling about leaving my entire life behind? Am I just a puppy to you? Trailing you around with drool around his jowls? What if I didn't want to leave the dome, did you ever think of that? Your excitement is frustrating. You clearly have no regard for how someone else might be feeling."

Celia's anger was building with every word spewed from his mouth as she watched him pace until finally, she couldn't take it anymore.

"Just shut up!" She shouted.

Her outburst quieted him and she watched as he stared at her.

"It's not my fault my parents assigned you to me, and I will not apologize for it. I was in a great mood this morning Brody! This is all I've ever wanted, and you're ruining it!"

An uncomfortable silence marinated around them as the sounds of the forest came to the forefront. Little scuttlings in the distance and treetops swaying, their silken leaves whooshing against each other. Celia got tired of waiting for a response and took a step to keep on going. But Brody gently grabbed her elbow and tugged her around to look at him. Heat crawled up her belly and she felt her cheeks flush.

What is happening to me.

His heavy voice was soft. "I'm sorry. You're right. It just seems like you don't see me sometimes. Like I'm just another decoration on your mantle." He took a deep breath. "I'm happy I'm the one who gets to be here with you. Just don't forget that I'm a person too, okay?"

Nervous butterflies took flight from her toes to her chest and Celia was left rooted to the spot as Brody walked on without looking to see if she would follow. She shook off her surprise, her head swimming with a whiplash of emotion, and focused on putting one foot in front of the other.

What the hell was that?

She shook her head.

They arrived at Elijah's lone cabin in the woods. The purplish hue of his little log home filled Celia with all the comforts of familiarity. She saw Elijah watching through his front window, the dark curtains swayed as his face disappeared and he came running out his front door.

He rushed to Celia and wrapped her in a big bear hug lifting her feet off the ground as giant bouts of laughter echoed out of him.

Celia laughed in surprise. "Glad you're not mad about us invading your privacy." She choked out as he released his hold on her and placed her back on the ground.

"Not at all, sister!" He beamed with joy. "I can handle having two house guests, that's a perfectly reasonable number." His grin dropped as he turned in Brody's direction. He spoke directly to Brody, narrowing his gaze. "As long as we all keep our thoughts to ourselves."

Celia cleared her throat chasing away the awkwardness. She looped her arms through Elijah's and walked towards the cabin. "Hey, I'm sorry for the way I was acting the other day. I don't know what came over me. I was just so, overwhelmed, all of a sudden. Can you forgive me?"

Elijah pulled her tighter. "Nothing to forgive, we're all human right?"

He winked and Celia smiled. Spending time with her brother was exactly what she needed. She would rest today and tomorrow would begin her new journey. Would the people of Meraiis welcome her? Could she be the savior the Sanctuary needed? Celia did not know if being a liaison was the answer her people needed, but she would give it her all. There was a whole world waiting for her to explore, and she wondered what mysteries lie in waiting for her to discover.

Everything was about to change.

CHAPTER SIX

The excitement from yesterday was beginning to fade. Scared tension of the unknown plagued Celia now. She heard Elijah say something but his words were muffled.

What did he just say?

"Celia."

The room started to come into focus again. She was sitting on the couch next to Elijah in his cabin.

His voice was more clear this time. "Celia. Did you hear a word I just said?"

The fog dragged its clouded tentacles away and she could see clearly again. "Hmm? Oh, um, I'm sorry, Elijah. Can you say that again?"

Elijah let out an exasperated sigh and dropped his head into his hands. He ran his fingers through his red curly hair, then raised his bright blue eyes to look at her. "This is important, Celia. I was asking if you remembered where the boundary line is?"

Celia cleared her throat and forced a grin. "Yes, yes of course I remember." She gave a small nod to try to reassure him she was taking this seriously, but Elijah's face fell.

"Celia, you have to be vigilant. Stay within our boundaries and keep watch for the sentries. As soon as you see red, stop. Keep your distance. They'll know you're there and they'll come when they're ready." Elijah wiped his palms on his pant legs.

A flash of black struck Celia behind her eyes and her head swam. "Did you see that?"

Panic crossed Elijah's eyes. "See what?"

The colors swam in her vision again and this time they were joined with intense pressure in her frontal cortex.

Elijah was quiet but started to rub Celia's back in slow circles. "Let me get you some water."

Celia felt the couch move and cold creep in from where Elijah had gotten up. A few moments later he came back with a glass of cool liquid and handed it to her. Celia gulped the drink down and took a deep breath.

She handed the glass back to Elijah and he set it on the table in front of them. "Celia, I think you have a migraine. I can't be sure, your thoughts, they're all...muddled? Yes?"

When she did not say anything, he continued. "Maybe you should go tomorrow, rest today. You don't have to rush into this."

Celia sat up straight like a lightning rod had fused to her back. "No!" She saw the distressed look coming from Elijah, and relaxed. "I mean, no. I'm fine, it's passing already. I can't wait Elijah. I have to do it now, or I feel like I never will."

Elijah nodded his head. "I get that, I do. Sometimes you have to leap before you lose your nerve. But are you sure? It's only one day."

Celia tried to calm her nerves, and looked at him. "Yes, I'm sure. I feel better already and I'm sure some fresh air will do me some good."

She flashed a smile to nail in her reassurance, and it seemed to work. Elijah stood and led her to the front door.

Outside Brody was impatiently waiting. "Finally. What took you two so long? Are you ready to go?"

Elijah glared at him and Brody's shoulders tensed when he crossed his arms. Celia watched the two size each other up and she could see Elijah going into defensive big brother mode.

She didn't need the two arguing right now. She hurried between the pair and laughed. "Yeah, I'm ready. Why? Do you have somewhere better to be? Hot date that I'm making you late for?"

Elijah shook his head and went back inside without a word. Brody dropped his defensive stance and turned to walk ahead.

He grumbled about something that Celia couldn't hear. She hurried to catch up to his side and nudged his arm. "What was that? No smart-ass reply?"

Brody shrugged and took a step further away as he said. "Nothing. It's nothing. Just stay close and try to be quiet."

Celia scoffed. "Why? Are we going into battle?"

Brody stopped and turned to face her. "No, Celia. But it's not exactly safe out here, and what we're doing isn't exactly a friendly neighborhood meeting. It's a big deal and I wish you'd act like it."

Celia took a deep breath and let it out slowly. "Listen, Brody. I do take this seriously, more than you could possibly understand. I was just trying to lighten the mood. You've been so tense since we left. I'm sorry if you didn't want to be here with me. But that's not my fault, my parents made the assignment, you know that, right?"

Brody wouldn't look at her when he spoke. "Yeah, I know it wasn't you. It's not exactly like I left anything behind, but it hurt when you didn't take me into consideration at all, like I was just an accessory to you. You didn't even come to tell me you were leaving. It was just Téa coming to tell me about my new assignment. And you were in a horrible mood the other day. You usually come hang out with me every night, read together and just chill. But you didn't reach out at all, it feels like you're slipping away."

Celia took a step towards him and placed a hand on his arm. "I'm sorry Brody, really. You're right, I should have talked to you about wanting to leave. But I thought you'd be happy, because I am. I'm happy you're here."

Warmth spread up her abdomen, and she couldn't help but smile when Brody looked at her with hopeful eyes. Celia took a step closer and said. "Besides, it's nice having my best friend here with me for this."

Celia's stomach sunk along with Brody's smile, and the unease started to settle back in. "Friend, right." Brody said.

Nausea came next and Celia put an arm out to her side to steady herself.

Concern creased Brody's brow and he hurried to support her with his body. "Celia, are you okay?"

She tried to shake off the sudden wave of discontentment. She gripped his arm for strength and tried to keep the rolling waves of bile from surfacing.

"I haven't been myself lately. Ever since that meeting with my mom and the other council members... It's like my emotions are giving me whiplash. I can't see straight sometimes it's so overwhelming. I feel a little sick."

Brody helped Celia over to a smooth square ruby boulder and eased her down. She took a few more breaths and placed her shaking hands flat on the stone.

Brody lowered himself down next to Celia. "Do you want to go back? We're not exactly far, we could go tomorrow."

Celia shook her head. "No, just give me a minute okay?"

Brody nodded his head and sat quietly next to her. Celia took in their surroundings. A gentle breeze brushed her hair. There was a giant rainbow made of what she could only describe as netting, like a thick spiderweb stretched between two trees. It shimmered and swayed in the wind wafting a sweet floral scent in her direction.

Everything on this planet was designed to entice and trap its prey. The rainbow web with its mesmerizing colors and sickly-sweet scent was the home of an Ipsey. A squirrel-sized black rodent with dozens of eyes, colorful wings, and furry mouth pincers. Harmless to most, but deadly for any avian creature. It blinds anything that flies too close with its shiny wings and jumps nearly eight feet up to snag its prey with its pointed claws, using its mouth pincers to swallow the poor flying thing whole.

Even the silken purple plant life seemed like a comfort, but if the branches are too long and the wind too wild, those soft limbs will wrap themselves around a thing, like a giant suffocating rope in need of a good hacking.

When her breathing calmed, and the sick feeling went away, Celia pushed off the rock. "Come on, let's go."

Brody grabbed her backpack that she had set on the ground and started to help her put it on.

She stopped him. "I can put my own bag on, Brody." She smiled.

She took the bag and he backed away with a grin and hands up.

The pair continued their way to the closest outpost. While Elijah was the only civilian living outside the dome, there were half a dozen security stations along the perimeter of the Earth zone. Each with two permanent guards which were switched out every six months. It was considered an abundance of over-protection by most. Considering the people of Meraiis had no apparent desire to chase them away or breach the treaty line, and the Beast wars ended fifteen years ago. Plus, there hadn't been a soul invasion in just as long. But her mother insisted that the people from Earth never let their guard down.

The guards running the security stations were more like glorified lookouts. Each person assigned here had to do one year of perimeter security before they began their real security training inside the Sanctuary.

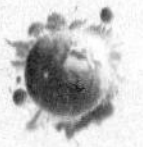

It was just after midday when they finally arrived at their destination. The outpost was an elaborate treehouse made with local materials. Brody climbed up the trunk which had stairs built into the wood part of the way, and pulled on a rope three times. Celia could hear the bell clanging above announcing their arrival. A guard at the top dropped a rolled-up ladder and it cascaded down towards them.

Celia went first. The ladder wiggled side to side with each step as she pulled herself up. Her hands were starting to hurt from where the wooden rungs dug into her palms. The weight of her backpack seemed heavier and heavier the longer she climbed.

Finally, huffing and puffing she pulled herself up into the treehouse on her hands and knees. She collapsed and rolled to her side laughing.

She could hear Brody breathing heavily as he sat next to her.

One of the guards addressed them. He looked about the same age as Celia, had bright blue eyes and buzzed blonde hair, his voice loud, cutting through the sound of her blood pulsating in her ears.

"Yeah, that climb is hard to get used to. Great for building muscle though!" He reached out a hand to Celia and she let him help her up. "I'm Carl, and this" he gestured to his left, "is Lucy."

Lucy was shorter than her and appeared in her early twenties. Her dyed purple hair was in a pixie cut and she had dark wide green eyes. She reached out a hand, and Celia shook it in greeting. "Thanks for having us."

They both smiled. "It's nice to have the company! It'll be good to have someone to talk to other than Carl here." Lucy spoke. "All he does is go on and on about how he misses his boyfriend." Lucy said in a singsong teasing voice and Carl blushed.

Carl interrupted, apparently eager to change the subject. "Let's give you the tour shall we?" He narrowed his eyes at Lucy as she laughed, and the group followed him inside. It was a short and easy tour. The treehouse had one open room with a small kitchen and sitting area, one bathroom, and one bedroom with two sets of bunk beds.

After Celia and Brody dropped their bags on their bunks, they all went to the front room.

Carl was in the kitchen making some late lunch for everyone of sandwiches and fresh fruit. Lucy was practically vibrating at the small table, her excitement was obvious.

Her high-pitched voice greeted them the moment they walked in the room. "So when do you make first contact? Do you think they'll show? Mrs. Garcia told us everything about you being the new liaison and all. Has the Sanctuary ever had a different liaison other than Mrs. Garcia? Do you–"

Carl cut her off. "Lucy, come on, they just got here. Can you contain yourself for like.. a minute?"

Lucy rolled her eyes. "Whatever, Carl. I know you're just as excited as I am. Nothing ever happens around here."

Carl snorted and kept busy in the kitchen. Celia was grinning as she watched the interaction. Lucy's enthusiasm was contagious.

Celia laughed. "It's okay. My mom, sorry, Mrs. Garcia, warned me that it could take a few days for them to respond, and she also warned me that they may not respond to me at all. But I think I'll head to the edge of the borderline tonight, maybe I'll get lucky and someone will respond by morning."

Brody's deep voice broke the silence. "Seriously Celia? Can you just wait a minute? Take just one night off. Let us get a good night's sleep. Once you go down there you can't leave until someone makes contact. I want to sleep in a bed at least tonight, please."

Silence spread throughout the room. Carl and Lucy both shifted uncomfortably as though they were intruders on a lovers quarrel.

Black flashed behind her eyes again and threatened to bring back the nausea from earlier. Celia tried to shake off the feeling of being uncomfortable in her own skin. Her words came out weak. "You're right. We'll sleep here tonight and set up our tents in the morning. If you'll excuse me."

Without another word, Celia went back to the bunk room. She lay down on one of the bottom beds and closed her eyes to try and get the room to stop spinning.

CHAPTER SEVEN

It had been three days of sleeping in separate tents next to the treaty line with Brody. Three days of Carl and Lucy dropping off supplies, careful to keep their distance so as to not spook any hidden Meraiin people. Three days of relieving themselves in the woods, and yet, there had been no response from the people of Meraiis... until now.

"Did you see that!?" Celia jumped up in enthusiasm. It was the first time she had felt anything resembling joy in days.

"See what?" Brody grumbled and rubbed his eyes.

"Aren't you supposed to be my guard?" Celia questioned. "You should be more alert, Brody."

Brody was warming up some soup in a pan over their small fire and set it down obviously frustrated. "I was just making us some food Celia, give me a break."

Celia huffed in indifference, and then pointed to a spot behind the treaty line roughly five yards away. "Look. Over there in that group of trees, I could have sworn I saw a sentry."

Celia crouched down as though that would improve her eyesight and whispered to herself. "I know I did."

Brody kneeled down beside her and looked in the direction Celia had pointed. "All I see is trees, Celia."

He stood back up and brushed his pants off. Celia shook her head and kept staring. Suddenly, there was movement in the group of trees, exactly where she had seen the sentry a moment ago. Slowly, a deer with a slight shimmer to its tawny coat emerged from its hiding spot. It made eye contact with Celia, pawed at the ground once, turned around, and walked back into the red forest.

Frozen with anticipation, Celia refused to peel her eyes away.

Where were the rest of the sentries?

The deer almost always traveled in a herd protecting the borderline and relaying messages. History says, according to the elders, that shortly after the people from Earth arrived on Meraiis the Earth deer turned their loyalty to the people of Meraiis. Their physiology had changed upon arrival in ways the elders could not explain. As a result, they were able to suck the air straight from the lungs of any living thing. They also were able to communicate telepathically with the people of Meraiis. They became their sentries. Protecting their newfound friends, the Meraiin.

"Brody!? Seriously, how did you not see that?" Celia stood and stretched her back for only a moment with her hands on her hips.

Brody went back to stirring the soup over the fire. "Celia, I think we've been out here too long and your hopes are too high. I didn't see anything."

Celia crossed her arms in irritation. "I'm going for a walk."

Brody stood swiftly. "I'm supposed to go with you, can it wait until after lunch?"

Celia waved him off and kept walking. "I'll be fine Brody, I'll be right back."

She did not wait for a response and walked faster to get away from the suffocation of despair. The further she got from camp, the lighter she felt. The air in her lungs came in easier and deeper. The feeling of frustration and sadness lessened. She missed the carefree version of herself and wondered where that version kept disappearing too.

She could no longer smell the hearty herbs in their soup, or hear the crackling of their fire, and still, she walked. Why is he such an ass lately? Celia wondered. He wasn't always that way. Brody used to be her best friend, her reading buddy, her confidant. But lately, he was just difficult to be around.

She wondered if maybe he was realizing that no matter how much her parents cared about him or supported him, they weren't his mom and dad. Training with the other guards day in and day out was most likely not very emotionally fulfilling. Perhaps it was the realities of adulthood that were bringing out this animosity in him. The rose-colored glasses of childhood had broken, and in their wake was the harsh light of reality.

Celia found an overturned log to sit on. Its normally dark purple timber faded to lavender, a sign of decay. She tested its firmness before sitting. The vegetation on Meraiis was softer and less dense than that of Earth, and when trees fell, they decayed more rapidly as they rotted from the inside out.

She wrapped her arms around herself, thinking. Once she had some space between herself and Brody, she realized there was no excuse for the way he had been treating her lately. He either needed to speak up with whatever his issue was, or get over it. Either way, it was not her burden to shoulder.

Deep in thought about the possibility of losing her oldest friend, Celia caught a whisper of a voice. The fine hairs along her arms and neck stood on end. A primal instinct deep within her came to life, alerting her to something before she was consciously aware of what it was.

"Celia."

"Who's there?" Celia stood up fast and turned in all directions.

"I'm not going to hurt you."

The voice sounded in her head, amplified like a loudspeaker echoing around her mind. Celia dug her nails into her palms preparing for the next onslaught.

"Come out where I can see you!"

"You need to leave, Celia. Tonight. Go home."

The voice had definition that time, it was masculine and perhaps empathetic?

"I will not leave. I need to speak to someone in charge, to-"

"No. You need to leave. Please."

Celia spun around looking for the source of the voice, but she found nothing. There was no sense of which direction the sound was coming from when the voice was flooded in her mind.

"The Meraiin people will not show when there is a threat nearby, you need to leave."

Celia pressed her palms to her ears, the thoughts that were not her own were so loud and disconcerting that it was difficult to concentrate.

"I am not a threat."

"Not you."

Celia pressed harder on her temple, bending over from the reverberating noise in her head.

"My people are not a threat. We just need to talk, please."

"Leave him, before it's too late."

She stood up straight as though the invisible force were about to attack, spinning around rapidly.

"Leave who!?" Celia shouted, but received no reply.

She stood for so long she was beginning to wonder if she imagined the whole thing. Perhaps her mind was betraying her. When little clouds of mist formed before her eyes, she realized it was her breath and that night had fallen.

She heard loud crashing footsteps swiftly approaching from behind her, but when she tried to turn around she realized her legs were stiff.

Brody came running out of the darkness, obvious panic written all over his face. "Where the hell have you been! Do you have any idea how worried I've been!?"

Celia tried to shake off the veil of fear that was overtaking her and stared directly at Brody. "Stop shouting at me

Brody, I'm not a child and you're not my father. I've only been gone for what? Maybe thirty minutes?"

Brody relaxed the gun he had been holding, letting it rest at his side as the muscles in his jaw danced in contempt. "Are you serious, Celia? Look around, it's dark, you've been gone for hours, I've been looking everywhere for you!"

She could not deny that she seemed to be missing time. She had left when the suns were high in the sky, and now she could see her skin illuminated in the bright light of the moons.

She tried to sound more confident than she felt as the unease moving within threatened to break her. "Let's just get back to camp, okay?"

Brody raised an arm to the air in anger. "Seriously? That's all you have to say. What were you doing out here?"

Celia stomped past him without making eye contact. "Just drop it, Brody. Let's go."

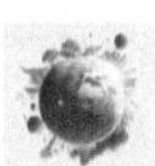

Celia awoke in the middle of the night with a start. Brody was in her tent, standing above her breathing deeply, unmoving.

Celia scurried to sit up. "What the hell, Brody!?"

He did not move or speak, just stood there, chest heaving, yet silent.

Her skin crawled, and her heart picked up pace, its beating rhythm like a hummingbird ready to take flight. She slowly eased her body around Brody's cemented feet. Celia carefully pulled on the zipper of the closed flap of the tent. Brody's heaving chest rose and fell and he continued his unmoving silent stance facing away from her.

Celia crawled out of the tent, and when her last leg was free she started to stand, and that's when Brody's ear-shattering and inhuman growl deafened her ears. The tent shook violently and Celia ran.

She pumped her legs as fast as she could, headed in the direction of the treehouse. Brody appeared suddenly from a darkened bush on her left, chasing after her, grunting like a wolf ready to take down his prey.

She switched direction so suddenly that she slipped on the ground, but caught herself before falling and ran faster-flinging dirt with her bare feet to get away from the predator that was supposed to be her best friend.

Brody was stronger. Faster. His super strength pushed him forward. She could feel his hot breath on her neck as she ran, she knew then, he was building up a fireball within him. For the first time she didn't think of his super strength and fireball ability as a benefit for their protection, instead, it was the weapon that would be used in her demise. She was seconds away from getting caught, or burned.

Just as his fingertips grazed her sides, a powerful yell of surprise shot at her from behind. She turned to look and Brody was hung from a tree by his ankle. Hanging upside down reaching his arms tirelessly, a futile attempt at grabbing her. An ugly growl persistent and hungry on his lips, eyes wild and devoid of the person she once knew.

Celia bent over gasping to catch her breath. Her whole body shook with the effort of holding back tears. Before she even had a thought of what to do next, the voice from earlier filled her mind.

"Come with me."

Celia spun around, looking for the source but finding nothing in the dark.

"Where are you?"

"I'm here, don't be frightened."

She clenched her fists. "Easier said than done. Who are you?"

"My name can not be understood in words, it is more of a feeling, but you may call me... Rees."

As her breathing calmed, Celia was anxious to get away from the growling that was still coming from Brody hanging above her but also torn about leaving him behind that way.

"Do not worry. Your other... friends will find him soon. Please come with me. I can help you."

Celia scoffed. "Help me? You're a disembodied voice, and you want me to trust you? I'm not going anywhere until you show yourself, and explain what the hell is going on!"

Celia heard a rustling to her left and jumped back while trying to avoid Brody's swinging arms. Slowly a dark figure emerged from the shadowed trees. He was cloaked in hooded heliotrope robes, she could not make out a face or features. The figure took a few more steps until he was a few feet away and bathed in the moonlight. He looked like the grim reaper come to steal her soul.

"Yeah, I'm not going anywhere with you buddy." Celia started to back away when she heard his commanding voice enter her mind again, this time with a hint of desperation.

"Wait. Please."

Rees lowered his hood exposing his face, and the only word that came to Celia's mind was, stunning. He was beautiful. Not unlike humans, but his skin was a dark iridescent color, he almost shimmered in the moonlight. Had it not been for that defining feature, he could have passed for human. His hair was black, wavy, and rested just above his shoulders. His eyes... were beautiful. They were violet, kind, and mesmerizing with thick dark lashes. As he walked closer, she could see he was a few inches taller than her and had well defined muscles.

He reached out a hand slowly. "Please, come with me."

Brody released another deafening hungry yowl and Celia jumped towards Rees. He grabbed her hand and quickly pulled her away into the night.

Chapter Eight

Five minutes into their trek away from Brody, Celia started to panic. *What am I doing?*

She stopped mid-stride. "Wait a second. Where exactly are we going?"

Rees did not reply, he kept moving forward.

Celia spoke up louder this time. "I said, where are we going?" Silence. "I appreciate the help and all back there. I'm assuming you set the trap for, Brody? Or maybe it was already out there?"

Rees still did not answer and continued navigating his way expertly through the darkened forest. Avoiding fallen branches, ducking under low-hanging ones, all almost completely soundlessly and without pause.

Celia rushed to catch up, tripping and crashing through the undergrowth clearly inexperienced in the realm of stealth. She reached out a hand to grab his arm when he suddenly stopped.

"We do not touch unless permission is granted."

His voice sounded in her mind, and warmth flooded her cheeks. She wouldn't exactly want someone grabbing her arm without permission either, but the natural reaction of stopping someone who was not listening to her was so ingrained in her personality that she hadn't thought about respecting another person's boundaries.

She also realized that the booming telepathy had eased into natural conversation. Sure his voice was still loud in her mind. But it no longer echoed off her proverbial walls or reverberated down her spine.

She was getting used to it.

She gave her head a small shake. "You're right, I'm sorry." She paused and furrowed her brow. "Wait, how did you know I was going to grab your arm? Do you have eyes in the back of your head?"

"We do not only speak telepathically, I am fully in your thoughts."

Celia shivered. "And you're lecturing me about boundaries?"

Rees continued walking without answering and Celia stumbled along. "Look. You really need to tell me where we're going, or I'm going to turn back around. I shouldn't be outside the treaty line, you and I both know it."

"The choice is yours, but I feel obligated to warn you of the shadows, you will not rid yourself of them without help."

A chill ran up Celia's neck and she hesitated in her next steps to allow herself to think, but Rees kept going, so she hurried to stay in pace with him. "What do you mean shadows?"

Rees did not answer. Celia's breathing was coming out in big huffs and puffs trying to keep up, Rees's long legs and taller form.

Celia's irritation amplified with each unanswered question. She was following a stranger into Meraiis territory and no one knew where she was. *This is stupid, really stupid, I should go back.*

"You following me isn't stupid, it was I who saved you from the sentries those days ago."

Celia audibly gasped and had to stop to catch her breath. She stood with her hands on her hips staring at his back and finally, for once, Rees waited for her.

"I knew it! I thought I recognized you."

He turned around and Celia was taken by his dark iridescent skin, muscular physique, and violet eyes partially hidden by his black thick hair. They stood staring at one another under the light of moons. She could hardly see his chest moving at all while hers raged with the task of getting air back into her lungs.

When her breathing steadied, she asked. "Why? Why are you helping me?"

"Because it is the right thing to do."

Why did her anticipation deflate at that answer? What did she expect him to say? That he was overwhelmed by her beauty and overcome with the desire to save her? Stupid human hormones.

Ahem. "We should keep moving."

Embarrassment flooded her core and she had the sudden urge to run and hide. Keeping her thoughts quiet would take some getting used to.

"You have no need to hide your thoughts from me. You simply need to state that you no longer give me permission and I'll end our mental link. It is a courtesy I would be happy to oblige you. But considering we don't know each other's languages, we also would not be able to communicate. The choice is yours."

Uncertainty riddled Celia's mind. She definitely did not want some mega hot Meraiin hero guy invading her thoughts, but she also couldn't handle not being able to communicate with him.

"It's okay. Just know that I don't have control over my thoughts all the time, so don't read too much into them alright?"

"I understand. Humans are fleeting in their thoughts. Careless of the long-term repercussions."

Celia flustered and whatever attraction she had for him was ebbing away, replaced with indigent irritation.

"Wow! Okay, rude and judgmental much?"

"Only if you interpret my comment that way. It was simply an observation."

Anger flared up her sides. Celia planted her feet firmly and crossed her arms. "Look, Rees, I'm not here for your insinuating insults. I'm here for answers, which you will give me."

"You are not in a position to make demands. However, I am reasonable and will honor your request in exchange for a promise."

"A promise?"

"Yes."

Celia was unsure that she should be making promises to herself, let alone anyone else. Perhaps Rees had a point, humans had a fleeting nature. "Maybe, what's the promise?"

"You must promise you won't leave me."

An involuntary and tingly pleasantness ran up her limbs. Betrayed by her body, she could not help how nice the idea of promising to stay by his side felt. Celia actively tried to redirect her thoughts to those of a more tactical parliamentarian instead of those of a girl who lived a sheltered life within the pages of romance, fantasy, and adventure novels. Besides, she effectively achieved her goal of being liaison if she promised not to leave the side of a Meraiin.

"Okay, I promise I won't leave you. Now will you please tell me where we're going?"

Rees nodded as if satisfied, turned back around to continue walking away, and said. "To the Beasts."

Fuck.

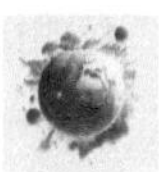

What the hell was she thinking? How serious were the repercussions of breaking a promise? With a human it just meant disappointment, but with the Meraiin people she had no way of knowing, would it mean war?

She expected Rees to give her some kind of answer in response to her flood of thoughts, but he said nothing. Geez she really messed up. Why the heck did her parents agree to let her do this? Because you're a mature twenty-year-old female. You can handle this. Pull your shit together woman.

"Listen, Rees. I'll honor the promise, but surely you can't be serious about going to Beast territory? It's suicide."

"Suicide is not a word we take lightly on this planet. I respectfully request you not use that term again."

Every mis-step, every slip of the tongue was chasing Celia further and further down into her cave of insecurity.

She tried to reign in some emotional strength to keep from metaphorically hiding. "What I meant to say, is that it's very dangerous and not smart at all to go to the Beasts. Why would we go there?"

"It's my home."

Celia's panic flared up again into a frenzy, she really messed up. How could she have messed up this badly? "What do you mean Beast territory is your home? You aren't a civilian of the Capitol? Are you even a Meraiin?"

"Of course I'm a Meraiin." Celia rarely detected any emotion from Rees, but this time she could sense the accusatory tone in his reply. Rees continued. "I was banished many years ago. The Beasts took me in."

Celia wanted to react in anger. She hadn't even accomplished her basic goal of becoming liaison for her people. She couldn't fulfill her duty with someone who wasn't even allowed within Capitol walls. Not only that, but why exactly was he banished? She could be following a dangerous criminal literally into the Beast's den!

But something about having Rees in her head made him much more present, real, and important than any job could be at this moment. And Celia felt deep down that he was not dangerous. He had saved her twice already. She would still figure out a way to help the Sanctuary expand. But for now, hearing the sadness in his reply as she continued to watch his back, she could not deny the compassion she felt for him.

She took a few long strides to catch up to his side and tripped again, landing face first onto the ground. She spit out a mouthful of dirt. She couldn't keep going like this. As much as she didn't want to admit it, she needed his help, and she asked. "May I hold your hand?"

Celia sensed the surprise and then joy coming from Rees at her request. She felt pleased at choosing compassion in a moment where she could have easily and justifiably chosen anger. Aunt Annabelle would be proud. Celia smiled to herself.

"Yes, I would like that."

Celia slowly intertwined her fingers through Rees's. His hand was warm despite the chill in the air. Rough and strong, it was obvious he was used to working in some way with his hands. And the happiness she sensed coming from him brought a smile to her lips.

"So. How much further do we have to walk?"

"We should be there by morning."

Celia was unsure about asking her next question. But self preservation pushed it from her mouth. "Rees? Do you know about the evil souls that Earth beings brought with us to Meraiis? Haven't you ever heard of the Beast Wars? It really is not smart or safe for me to go there with you. You've got to give me something?"

"Is it customary for Earthlings to give each other gifts in exchange for doing things one does not want to do?"

Celia snorted and laughed in surprise, "What? No." Well technically, yes. There were the jobs that people hated but had to do anyway in order to get their share of necessities. But that was not the point. "That's not what I meant. I didn't mean an actual thing. I just meant that I need you to give me some answers. I'm taking a lot of risk here by not running the other way."

"Ah. I see. Well many years ago the Beasts discovered a way to protect themselves from possession. The souls haven't invaded their territory for some time now. The Beasts took me in when I had nowhere else to go. They are my family."

Celia could not deny that hearing Rees's explanation was comforting. It did not appear that he was leading her into danger. Maybe all those adventure novels would come in handy after all by giving her the strength she needed to walk into the unknown.

"And you're sure the Beasts won't kill me?"

"Not on purpose."

"Ah. Well, that's comforting." She said.

"I'm glad that's a comfort for you."

"I was being sarcastic."

"I was too." Rees paused holding her still with their con-joined hands and winked at her, then continued leading the way.

Celia looked away trying to hide the pink in her cheeks. Butterflies fluttered around inside her when he gave her hand a squeeze.

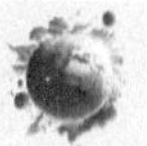

They had been walking all night hand in hand at a much slower pace. The suns were beginning to rise and awakened the sleeping creatures of the forest. Still unseen, but could be heard. Little squeals, gentle chirruping's, and distant howls sounded around them.

Something rustled near Celia's feet and she jumped closer to Rees. "Is there anything poisonous in this area? We still know so little of this planet. Our territory is so small."

"Anything poisonous?... Yes, and also no. A better answer is that you are not currently in harm's way."

Celia chuffed. "Well that's not entirely comforting, but thanks."

"It's customary for the requestor to release physical con-tact."

"Hmm?" Then the realization hit Celia, she was the one who asked to hold his hand and they had been doing so all night. "Oh my gosh! I'm so sorry, I didn't realize." Here came the familiar embarrassment worming its way into her belly.

"No apologies necessary. I enjoyed the connection."

Now a different kind of warmth was spreading within her. Get ahold of yourself Celia!

"Do you require assistance?"

"What?" Get ahold of yourself. "Oh no. Thank you, I'm fine. Just a lot to take in, you know?"

"No."

Oy vey.

Celia noticed the florals around them growing in number and size. Each petal contained an array of colors. She had never seen plant life like this before. Where the normal vegetation on Meraiis was soft and silken, these florals were sharp and firm. They didn't sway in the breeze, but their colors did dance in the sun. Like living mirrors reflecting off the light and shouting their hues to the world.

It was breathtaking.

The flowers got bigger and bigger and it was becoming difficult to avoid their dark indigo leaves. Before long they were taller than her and so close together that she was forced to stop.

Rees looked at her before saying. "Don't worry, they look sharp, but they will not cut you... Well-these kind won't."

Celia stared open mouthed at him. "You are terrible at comforting people you know that?"

"I did not know it was my responsibility to comfort you."

"It's-" She cleared her throat and shook her head. "It's not your job to comfort me."

"You are very focused on jobs."

Celia stopped and faced him, Rees stopped and stared back. "You are very literal."

"Words have meaning. They are important and must be treated with respect."

"Well, you've got me there."

Rees looked forward again. "We're here."

CHAPTER NINE

The colorful flora, twice as tall as Celia, shifted. They parted and moved in the ground tearing up the forest floor as they went, to allow her and Rees to pass. It took Celia's breath away and she stared with her mouth hanging open at the sight before her.

Once the path was clear Rees walked forward while Celia was rooted to the spot. The flowers puffed out little clouds of what Celia could only assume was black pollen.

"Are you coming?"

"This is incredible. Can all the plants on Meraiis do this? I've never seen anything like this before." She rubbed some of the dust between her fingers creating little streaks like ash between her palms.

Rees paused to turn and look at her. "Your eyes witness so much, yet you see so little."

Celia wrinkled her brow. "What exactly is that supposed to mean?"

"Have you never noticed the stark difference in vegetation in your Earth territory and the Meraiin border?"

Celia put her hands on her hips, she did not appreciate being spoken to like a child. "Well, yeah, but I thought that was artificially created to keep our territories distinct."

Rees shook his head. "It's so obvious is it not?"

Celia could only stare at him, she wasn't sure what point he was trying to make, and desperately wanted to say something snarky in response to his condescending attitude, but she also wanted to understand what he was trying to tell her. So she waited and listened.

Rees took a deep breath before explaining. "The arrival of your species and your small slice of Earth forced many of the indigenous Meraiis plant life in the surrounding area to evolve. They cross-pollinated and some died out, but some survived and created the resulting color shift. Many of the animals had to flee the immediate area as their food sources died out or became inedible. Your Earth animals and plant life slowly found their way out of your dome and settled around the immediate area of the Sanctuary.

Celia furrowed her brow. "Then why do you allow us to stay?"

The Meraiin people allowed you to stay because we are not a violent species and your kind was minimally evasive as long as you were kept within your territory."

Celia nodded. "That makes a lot of sense. It is kind of obvious once you think about it. Bringing an entire piece of Earth with us to a new planet was bound to have some repercussions."

Celia thought to herself. I wonder why it's not talked about more? The effect our arrival had on Meraiis was not entirely positive. I wonder if we could leave the Sanctuary behind and completely adapt to Meraiis outside the dome?

Rees laughed. "Earthlings are so narcissistic, thinking only of themselves. It is highly unlikely that you will be able to negotiate more space. It is not in the best interest of Meraiis."

A flame of irritation ignited within Celia. She crossed her arms and scoffed. "It's called survival Rees. What's the alternative? We all die out? Earth goes completely extinct? The Dome and everything in it, is all that remains." She said passionately as she talked with her hands. "We're an endangered species! Don't the Meraiin people care about that?"

"The Meraiin do not intervene." Rees turned and kept walking forward without waiting for Celia's rebuttal. "Come, we must get out of the Cinis."

Celia furrowed her brow. "Cinis? Is that what this pollen is called? Will it hurt us?" She asked as she followed Rees.

"Only if you're an evil soul."

Celia took a step forward and the giant flowers behind her slowly moved back into place closing the gap simultaneously blocking her exit, which caused a flutter of panic within her chest. They were headed straight for the Beasts, and no matter how unworried Rees seemed to be, he was still a stranger and every bit of her history taught her that the Beasts were dangerous.

"They don't like being called Beasts. I only used that term for your benefit so that you could understand, but it is very much an insult."

Celia made a mental note to try harder not to let her mind wander into a frenzy. It was something to get used to, having someone else inside her head in such a present way. It was much more invasive and constant than the soulmate connection. Which with that connection, only emotions were sensed. Not her literal thoughts.

"What are they called then?" She asked.

"Their species are called Aniimarus, but they preferred to be called by their individual names. They are just as intelligent as you or I. Their physiology made them easy to possess, and when the evil souls discovered they could not inhabit humans on this planet, the Aniimarus became the most desired targets. As a result of your 'Beast Wars,' they are even more endangered than Earthlings."

Guilt started to crawl its way through Celia's gut. She had only ever been taught about how great her people were for defeating the beasts, she hadn't ever thought about them being victims of the battles. But of course, they would not have wanted to be possessed by a foreign entity and forced to fight and kill.

Who would want that?

The shame of her people's history as vicious killers overwhelmed Celia. A memory flashed through her mind of a time when she had to smoosh a bug inside her home, she had cried after killing it, and that was only a bug. The idea of taking the life of another living creature, with a soul and a mind of its own, made her sick to her stomach and heart ache. Bile rose in her throat but she fought it back down. The world around her spun.

For the first time, Rees had a reaction, what was it? He looked worried, concerned for Celia's wellbeing. His apparent care for her was a surprise, but not enough to shock her out of the despair tunnel she was falling down.

"Celia! Do not despair. Stay strong. Your elder's history is not your own. You can make better choices for your future generations."

Celia reached an arm out, looking for something to hold on to. Rees gently placed his arm under hers to keep her standing upright. Warmth blossomed at his touch and she found her reflection in his violet eyes. She tried to chase the feelings from her thoughts, it was hard not to feel the way she was. Being in close proximity to Rees, made all sound reason and logic float away. She could only focus on his arm wrapping around her waist and keeping her steady, the way he was strong but careful with her.

She suddenly felt very woozy and tried to shake the feeling off but only succeeded in wobbling against Rees.

"I had forgotten how much sleep you Earth beings need. It's almost morning and you have not slept. Come, let me carry you."

Those words shot adrenaline through her veins and Celia found her second wind. "I can walk on my own just fine, thank you very much." She said with more authority than she felt.

The combination of running away from Brody, walking through the forest all night, learning so many new things from Rees, and having not slept since the previous night was undeniably catching up to her, but Celia refused to be a damsel in distress. She would walk on her own two feet, meet the Aniimarus, and then pray they gave her somewhere to rest. Because no matter how determined she was to make a strong appearance, she could not keep standing much longer.

Damn it, he just heard all of that.

Rees laughed and Celia tried hard to keep the pink from her cheeks. "Can you at least pretend to stay out of my head?"

"It's impossible, it would be like you turning off your beating heart."

Celia froze, feet firmly planted, jaw clenched tight. "You mean to tell me, that your offer last night to turn our linked thoughts off was a lie?"

"Not exactly a lie. More of a bridge of perceived hospitality. But, yes."

"Do you have any idea how creepy that is?"

"No."

Celia wanted to shout so many things at him, but she could hear activity on the other side of the last batch of flowers and did not want to meet the Aniimarus for the first time by fighting with their adopted son. Plus, she had to admit to herself that she could use a minute to calm down anyway. They were literally from two different worlds and for all she knew he was considered reserved for his kind.

"We need to have a conversation about this at some point."

"It is only communication. Physical boundaries are of the only importance."

"Not to me. Mental and emotional boundaries are important as well."

"As you wish. Come, meet my family."

The final tall flowers spread out of the way revealing the Aniimarus village. Before them was a glistening blue floor, like dark water turned to solid gel, yet spongey to walk on. Light blue tree roots grew into alcoves dotted all around. Like giant veins that sprouted out of the ground, then grew and twisted themselves into many cave-like homes.

Their dwellings were one with Meraiis. Nothing looked built, it was grown into the shapes and sizes the Aniimarus needed. Colorful and shimmering butterflies flew in the thousands everywhere, but when they landed they curled up into a little ball just like a rolie polie with a snail-like bottom stuck to the trees.

"Those are called, Paliios. We whisper our needs to them and they talk to the trees for us. They are the conductors of the village, getting the roots to grow out their veins the way we need to create our homes."

Just then a dozen of them fluttered towards Celia and she stretched out her arms, twirling and laughing as they breezed around her.

"They're beautiful."

They smelled fruity like some kind of citrus, and when she looked closer they had tiny furry faces like that of a moth. She could see no mouth, but if she had to guess she would say they were tweeting as a bird would.

"They have welcomed you."

Rees was smiling at her and Celia's stomach did that flip-floppy thing that she had no control over.

Suddenly one of the trees moved close to her right side and she jumped in surprise when she realized it was not a tree, but an Aniimarus. It reminded her of a giant, light blue, bigfoot, like the ones that she read about in her book, "Mythical Monsters and Their Believers". It was standing upright and covered head to toe in a thick fur. Its emerald green eyes reflected the light and when it smiled she saw its sharp pointed teeth.

"He, is not an 'it'. His name is Oisin, my father."

A deep rumbling sound shook the leaves on the ground and Celia's eyes widened in terror.

"Celia, it's okay, he's only laughing."

Celia forced herself to look at Oisin's face and she saw that Rees was right. Oisin's laughter was loud and boisterous.

Why is he laughing at me?

"Because you nearly flew to the sky when he surprised you. It was funny." Rees shrugged his shoulders and smiled. He then started talking to Oisin out loud.

The Aniimarus language was like nothing Celia had ever heard before. She likened their voices to rolling thunder with waves of quiet with the occasional clash. Celia watched in fascination while the two conversed, wishing she could understand what they were saying.

Oisin turned and walked away gesturing with his arm for them to follow.

"He wants you to have breakfast with us. You can meet my mother and brothers." Rees's eyes lit up when he mentioned his brothers.

As they walked through the village with the rising suns, other Aniimarus peeked out from their dwellings, stealing glances at Celia. They were all various shades of blue, all with various shades of dark green eyes that reflected the light. The shorter ones appeared darker blue and the taller ones were a lighter blue. Celia assumed it was age-related, the shorter Aniimarus must be younglings. A couple of them had changed their course as Celia walked towards them, it was obvious they did not want to get too close to her.

As she saw more of them, she saw many seemed afraid of her. She hadn't noticed right away, their faces too foreign to be read easily. But as she saw more and more of what was clearly fear, she had the overwhelming desire to run out of the village. She felt like a trespasser, like she did not belong here, but she forced her feet to keep moving. One foot in front of the other, staying close to Rees, she was surprised by the urge to hold onto his arm, but Celia refrained.

Following Oisin as he expertly zig-zagged his way through the web of tree roots, Celia's anticipation amped up. She was in a foreign land, surrounded by creatures she thought only yesterday would destroy her given the chance, come to find out they were more afraid of her. What was she doing here? She needed to get back to the Sanctuary. She needed to find out what happened to Brody. She was suddenly panicked by the thought of him hurting Carl and Lucy, and felt guilty for not thinking of them sooner.

"Celia, please try not to worry. Your friends are safe, I promise. Rest here for a while, I can explain more after you've had something to eat and have slept for a few hours. You wouldn't make it home in your current physical state."

She balked at the notion. "And how would you know? You don't know what I'm capable of." She secretly knew he was right even if she did not want to admit it, and then remembered that he knew her every thought, and blushed.

"Celia, I am not judging you. Please allow me to help you. There's much more happening on this planet than you realize."

Celia bit back the question of what exactly Rees meant by that and tried to focus on enjoying witnessing so many new things. The way the red sun streamed through the gaps in the canopy above and lit up the wings of the Paliios, even the Aniimarus fur shone in the light.

Oisin came to a stop in front of a curtain of skinny dangling vines that acted as a doorway. He pushed them aside and walked through. The loud thundering of their language exploded as Celia followed him and Rees inside. Two shorter Aniimarus and another taller one all embraced Oisin and Rees hugging each other laughing their rumbling sounds.

"Celia, I'd like you to meet my mother and my brothers." He gestured around the room, "Aoife, Padraig, and Darragh."

Celia smiled and nodded as Rees beamed around the room, a proud son returned to his family. His mother, Aoife, two feet taller than Celia, suddenly pulled her close. She wrapped her large furry arms tightly around Celia dancing side to side as deep rumblings purred out of her.

Rees laughed. "She's happy to meet you."

"I gathered that." Celia smiled as Aoife released her and gestured to what must be their kitchen table.

It was a large, about five feet across, round cut off tree trunk. So light blue that it almost looked white. It was loaded with a variety of foods that Celia had never seen before. Green ovals with pink spikes cut into quarters. Something that appeared moist, flat, circular, and pink. Yellow rectangular blocks, and more that Celia could never venture as to guess what they were.

Rees leaned in close to her ear and whispered his language while translating in her mind. She found that she liked the sound of his voice even more when it came from his mouth and not his mind. "All local fruits and vegetables, it is safe to eat." His language was different from that of the Aniimarus, gentle and flowing like a stream without pause, occasional tinkling sounds like a bell; beautiful.

Celia shivered pleasantly at the closeness before he walked away and took a seat on the blue gel-like spongy floor facing the table.

Everyone dug in laughing and talking as they ate with their hands. Celia hesitantly picked at her food, but when she took her first bite her mouth was flooded with flavor. The purest and most fresh fruit she had ever eaten. It splashed her tongue and tickled her senses. Her eyes widened and she took bigger bites chewing and smiling as she tried and failed to follow the conversation at the table.

Afterward, Rees brought her to a waist height rectangle tower weaved from plants against the wall. A Paliios was perched on the edge. Rees whispered his language to it, and it fluttered up and landed on a long vine hanging from the ceiling. Suddenly a steady trickle of water flowed out of the vine into the rectangle.

"Here, wash your hands. The water has natural antimicrobials in it."

Fascinating. Celia thought. Rubbing her hands slowly together under the water she was surprised to find that it was warm. Between the warmth washing over her, and Rees's calming presence next to her, sleep deprivation overcame her. Her eyes drooped and her head nodded, she was finding it hard to stay upright.

"Hold on, I have you."

Rees lifted her off her feet. Celia wanted to protest, but after forty hours of being awake, the lull of sleep was overtaking her. Rees carried her in his arms through the den and into a smaller alcove where there was a bed shaped like a Paliios, made from the same blue plant life as the rest of the village. He gently placed her down. She forced her eyes to take in one last glimpse of him as he left the room and her heart fluttered as she fell into a deep sleep.

Chapter Ten

Rain slammed against the windows. Hail ricocheted off the tin roof of the barn and lightning lit up the sky. The barn, more like her second home, had a sitting area, and burning logs in the fireplace, but something else gave the space an eerie glow. Celia pulled her blanket tighter, the bales of hay poking through her clothes, she shifted uncomfortably. The horses neighed in agitation, flicking their tails. A dark shadow pooled under the barndoor and slinked towards her. The shadow slowly took shape and stood before her. It stretched its mouth and reached for her. She leaned away and its shadowy arms got closer and closer...

Celia woke with a start, gasping for breath and taking in her surroundings. It took her a moment to remember where she was and why she was there. The deep rumbles and clashing sound of the Aniimarus language reached her ears. Those sounds explained the thunderstorm in her dream, but not the creepy shadow man, and it was hard to shake the unease, her skin still crawled.

The talking ceased and all was quiet for a moment before Celia saw the outline of Rees on the other side of the hanging vines that acted as a door. He did not enter the alcove but spoke to her through his telepathy.

"You've had a nightmare, may I enter?"

Celia gulped. "Yes."

She was surprised by the concern etched in his face.

"Are you okay? Can I get you anything?"

Celia cleared her throat. "Some water?"

Rees left without a response and was back in seconds. He carried something that looked like a smooth purple coconut with a hole in the top. He handed it to her and she cautiously took a sip. It had a faint taste to it, like cucumber water with a hint of floral.

"It's good. Is this just water? Or is there something in it?"

"May I sit next to you?"

Celia's heart skipped a beat. "Yes." Warmth flooded through her when he sat next to her. She hoped he couldn't hear her racing heart and then blushed when she knew he would hear that thought, and tried to focus only on his words while staring at her feet.

"In this village, there are seven flowing waters carried here from all around the globe. Different parts of this planet have different ecosystems and different plant life. Much like how your Earth was."

Celia squinted her eyes and looked up at him. "How do you know so much about Earth?" His violet gaze was directed at her, an involuntary sensual shiver took her breath away, she tried to hide her thoughts.

Rees did not answer her question but kept talking about the waters. "The different plants have different elemental properties as a result of flowing through the various biomes. So, to answer your question, no, there is nothing added to this water, but, yes, it does have 'something' in it. This one aids in mental health, easing anxiety, and similarly related ailments."

Celia was so entranced by his words she did not realize the silence that had permeated the room. She shifted next to him to put a small gap between them to calm her racing heart.

"Fascinating." She said before taking another drink.

"It is time for you to go home before a war is started."

Celia coughed, spraying water on the ground. "What war?" Her eyes were wide, and her heart raced full of panic.

"Your mother and father believe the Meraiin people have kidnapped you."

"What?" Celia shot up, her voice a high-pitched squeal. "How do you know this?"

"Here." He gestured to the corner of the bed. "The Paliios weaved a tunic for you, and Aoife knitted you some leaf shoes. Aoife cleansed your wounded feet while you slept. I'll leave, so you may dress."

She glanced at the clothes, heart racing, she tried not to shout. "No. Don't leave yet. How do you know this? What happened?"

"Brody's possession ended shortly after we fled. Carl and Lucy found him hanging from his feet with no memory and you were missing. They assumed the worst and told your parents. They are preparing to invade."

"Crap on a cracker! We've got to go, now!"

Rees did not move right away but started laughing.

"What about this situation is funny?"

"Crap on a cracker?" He shook his head, continuing his laughter as he exited the room.

After he left, Celia gingerly touched the bottom of her feet. She expected them to be torn up after all the hours she spent walking barefoot, but was surprised to find them almost completely healed. Her pajamas that she'd been wearing were ripped and barely hanging on in some places, so she was grateful for the tunic as well.

Celia allowed herself a brief moment to appreciate the magical quality of this place, and hoped she would have a chance to return someday. But with her family on her mind, she hurriedly got changed and rushed out of the room.

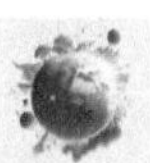

Oisin, Aoife, Padraig, and Darragh were waiting for them in the front alcove. Aoife was smiling, her pointed teeth shining, dark green eyes gleaming. She held out a medium-sized bag weaved from plants. Rees did not reach for it, he looked from Celia to the bag and tilted his head, Celia got the hint and reached for the bag with a smile and a nod.

Aoife pulled her into another of her great fuzzy hugs swinging her from side to side. It was hard not to smile, but the panicked frenzy was still at the forefront of her mind. Oisin patted Rees on the back. Padraig and Darragh enveloped him in a group hug.

Celia shifted her weight side to side, in a hurry to leave, and nearly sprinted outside when Rees gestured an arm towards the exit indicating that he was ready. After tripping for the third time, over the large tree roots that wound their way around the blue gel sponge ground, Celia reluctantly slowed down and allowed Rees to take the lead.

When they reached the tall stalks of flowers, Celia paused to take one last look at the Aniimarus village and colorful fluttering Paliios, then turned to leave, in a hurry to reach her family and prevent a war.

They had been walking for roughly four hours judging by the alignment of the suns when Celia relented and admitted that she needed a momentary rest. Before she even had a chance to say anything, Rees took a seat on a fallen log, and Celia sat next to him. She was getting used to him knowing her every thought and admitted to herself that it was kind of nice.

Unlike her soulmate link with her father, Rees actually knew what she was thinking. Her father could sense her emotions and she could sense his in return, but he often misinterpreted the meaning behind them. Always making assumptions and rarely giving her a chance to speak her mind. It was partly why she was so grateful for the close relationship she had with her mother.

Her mom always asked how she was feeling and gave her the space to answer. Lately, her emotions hadn't seemed like her own, so out of place from her normal. She was reminded of her attitude and behavior towards her mother not so long ago and was baffled at where all that resentment and hate had been coming from. That, and the weird attraction feelings she had been having towards Brody even though she had always only ever cared for him as a best friend.

"The answer is right there waiting for you, yet still you do not see it." Rees said, shaking his head.

"What is that supposed to mean?" Celia sat up straight and crossed her arms. "What am I missing?"

Rees stood, took a step away from her, and gently spoke his melodic language while translating in her mind. "You are absorbing the emotions of the people around you."

Just then it was as if a light bulb was turned on. The final puzzle piece slipped easily into place. She shot up from the log. "Holy shit, you're right! It makes so much sense." Celia began to pace back and forth as she spoke. "The meeting with my mom and all those douchey leaders spewing their judgy negativity. I can't believe I didn't see it." She paused and gasped. "Oh my God, Brody, he's totally in love with me. He's festering inside with unrequited love. No wonder he's so bossy and angry all the time." She paused and pointed a finger in frustration. "No!" She dropped her hand and looked to the sky. After a few deep breaths she put her hands on her hips and shook her head. "That gives him no excuse for his behavior lately, the way he's been talking to me and trying to control me, it's ridiculous. That's not love!"

"It's not all his fault, the evil soul has been attempting to possess him for some time. They never gave up attempting to take over humans after the end of the War. Brody was their first success and now they won't stop. They're forming a wide-scale attack."

Celia spun to face him, eyes wild. "How do you know all of this!? Is there anything else you should be telling me?"

"No. Well yes. Your soulmate connection with your father isn't actually a soulmate connection like what your mother and aunt had. It was merely one of your fathers supernatural abilities that presented like a soulmate connection."

Well, that was a lot to process.

Celia crossed her arms again. "You know Rees, I've asked a few times and you've yet to answer. How do you know all this? About what's happening at the Sanctuary, and my father. Don't you trust me? I thought we... maybe... well, never mind." She said as she shook her head and marched forward.

"That's the wrong way."

Celia huffed, changed course, and stalked forward.

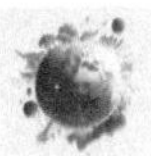

They continued the rest of their journey in silence. Celia tried to focus all her thoughts on their surroundings, trying extra diligently not to let Rees know what she was thinking. But it was harder said than done.

They were finally approaching the edge of the treaty line when Celia heard shouts in the distance. Thoughts of her family being brutally murdered flashed through her mind and she raced towards the noise. Fear and adrenaline coursed through her veins.

Celia burst through the tree line, staring in shock and fear at the scene that was unfolding before her. Her parents and a dozen Sanctuary members with the strongest abilities stood facing an army of at least one hundred Meraiin soldiers on foot, clad in their pliable suits of chameleon-like armor ready for attack.

Heart pumping and breath ragged Celia ran. She ran faster than she ever had in her life until she reached the border and hurtled herself at her mother and screamed.

"STOP!"

"Celia!?" Her mother wrapped her arms around her. "Where have you been?" She screeched. "What happened?" Her mother's tears escaped her. "I've been so worried!"

Guilt plagued her, she should not have left with Rees. "I'm so sorry mom. I'm so sorry."

Celia smoothed her mother's curly locks, no longer a child looking for comfort, but a daughter soothing her mother. Celia felt the fear then, the worry, and panic, and she could see it for the first time. She was absorbing her mother's emotions. But there was something else on the edge of those emotions, hitching a ride like a toxic parasite that could soon destroy them all.

Poison.

The same poison that used to eke out of humans on Earth through their evil deeds, was now collecting within Celia. She could sense it pool, feel it worming its way through her the longer she held onto her mother.

Celia jumped back in alarm. Confusion crossed her mother's face and Celia tried to project confidence despite the revelation inside of her, begging to come undone. "Tell the Sanctuary to stand down. The people of Meraiis had nothing to do with trapping Brody or my disappearance.

Téa nodded to her battalion commander and he gave the order to stand down. Celia then turned to Rees who was standing a few feet behind her, still hiding in the tree line. She spoke to him in her mind. "Can you translate for me?"

She could see him shake his head. "I told you, I was banished many years ago, they will not trust me. Remember, they can read your mind the same as I can. Just approach the borderline and speak your thoughts."

Celia nodded. "Thank you, Rees."

Rees smiled in acknowledgment and turned to leave, but Celia shouted in her mind. "Wait! Please don't go yet. Will you wait?"

"I can not, this is a journey you must take on your own." He said.

Celia shook her head. "Please."

There was only a moment of hesitation in his eyes before he said. "As you wish."

Comforted by knowing Rees was nearby waiting for her, she approached the borderline coming to a stop a mere foot from a Meraiin soldier. Their skin was pearlescent. Their bright orange eyes matched their short spiky hair, and when they spoke through telepathy their voice was feminine.

"Your people were seconds away from breaking our treaty. They accused us of kidnapping, this is a great insult to our people. We have been gracious enough to allow Earthlings to stay on our planet, but this is cause for reevaluation."

Celia's eyes widened in terror. "No, please, this has all been a huge misunderstanding. It will never happen again."

The Meraiin in front of her huffed in disbelief. "You can not possibly promise such a thing."

Celia stood fast, jaw set, and arms crossed. "I can promise that.. if... the Meraiin people approve me to become a liaison between our two species."

The Meraiin warrior looked as though she was considering Celia's words, so she pressed on. "If the Meraiin people would allow me to learn more about this planet, we could better understand each other. Instead of begrudgingly being neighbors, we could be allies."

The Meraiin laughed. "And why do we need you as an ally? We are far more powerful, we do not need Earthlings." She said the last word like an insult.

Celia narrowed her eyes. "I have it on good authority that the evil souls that followed us here have made progress in human possession. Earthlings are far more powerful than you realize, many of us have very strong abilities, and what do you suppose an evil soul could do with that kind of power?"

The Meraiin was quiet as she considered what Celia was saying.

Celia spoke one last time. "I know you are not naturally a violent species, and Earthlings do not want bloodshed either. Please, let us work together to face this threat."

The Meraiin sheathed a silver sword that Celia had just now noticed, but instead of hanging on a hip, the sword collapsed and folded itself into a small cube stuck to the inside of the Meraiin's gloved palm. "You make valid points, human. I am, Alva, master of war, and I approve your request."

Celia tried to contain her excitement from a successful negotiation by forcing back a smile. "I have one last request. I need a guide, someone who understands Meraiis, and who can help me through your planet."

Alva was about to reply when Celia kept talking. "I want Rees to be my guide, his banishment needs to be lifted."

At Celia's request, Rees made himself visible by walking out from behind the trees and moving to Celia's side.

"Redreesishual?" Alva shook her head. "No. This is impossible, his banishment cannot be undone."

Celia glared and infused more strength in her thoughts. "He alone knows how to defeat the evil souls, and he has been a great help to me. I must insist."

Alva stood her ground in silence before finally relenting. "Fine." Alva turned to walk away but continued to talk through her telepathy. "But his father, the King, will not be pleased. Come, we must get to the Capitol before nightfall."

Celia spun on her heel, mouth hanging open in surprise. "Seriously. You couldn't have mentioned that you're the son of the King?"

Rees looked to his feet and shrugged. "It is of no consequence once one is banished."

Celia saw her mother approach, twigs snapping underfoot. "Celia, what just happened?" She asked as she watched the Meraiin army retreat. "And who is this?" She asked while she looked at Rees.

Celia grabbed her mother's forearms and stared at her. "I'm so sorry mom, but I need to leave again."

Téa shook her head, despair seeped into her eyes. "No. I just got you back. You can't leave again."

"I have to, Mom. That Meraiin is their master of war, she has approved me to be a liaison between our two people. We need this. We need their Alliance for what's coming next."

Her mother gripped Celia back, a half embrace. "What do you mean? What's coming?"

Rees leaned toward Celia. "Give her the bag."

Celia had completely forgotten about the bag tied around her waist that Aoife had given her.

Seeing the question in her eyes, Rees said. "It is a bag of Cinis. If any of your people act violently or out of the ordinary while we are gone. Tell her to douse them in a small handful of the pollen. It is a short-term solution. We will need to plant Cinis blooms soon."

Celia nodded and turned back to her mother. "Mom, this is Rees. He's helping me." Celia looked toward Alva growing smaller in the distance. "I have to hurry. But listen, this is important. The evil souls are figuring out how to invade humans. This dust kills them. But use it sparingly. I'll be back soon. I promise." Celia pulled her mom into a hug and whispered in her ear. "I love you."

When she pulled back, Celia saw the tears well in her mother's eyes. "I love you too sweetheart."

Téa hesitated and looked behind her to the dozen of Sanctuary members. Among them were Carl, Lucy, and Brody. She motioned for them to join her. When Brody approached Celia could see what she guessed was embarrassment or regret hanging heavy on his shoulders. He couldn't even bring himself to look her in the eyes.

"I want these three to go with you. I'd feel better if some of our people were with you as well."

Celia started to form a rebuttal, but her mother cut her off. "Please. Do this for me, and be safe."

Seeing the worry in her mom's eyes, and knowing that Brody hadn't been himself lately, Celia reminded herself that he was her oldest friend. Besides, it wasn't just his guard training that was beneficial, but his abilities could come in handy as well. Celia grabbed a small handful of the Cinis from the bag and blew it in Brody's face.

Brody coughed and sputtered before raising his voice. "What the hell, Celia?"

Rees laughed behind her and Celia turned to look at him. "What?"

"I told you, he was no longer possessed."

"Whatever, better safe than sorry." Celia closed the bag of Cinis and gave it to her mother with one last hug. "See you soon."

Chapter Eleven

As her mother grew smaller in the distance, Celia was overwhelmed with the enormity of the task that stood before her. The future of the last remaining piece of Earth rested on her shoulders. But even as she acknowledged that responsibility, the ever more present threat of the revival of the evil souls loomed over her.

Brody walked behind her with Carl and Lucy, keeping his distance. Celia wondered how much of the past few days he really remembered because his shameful body language betrayed him. She doubted that he had no memory of attacking her.

Rees walked ahead of her. The longer she stared at his back, she realized something that was so obvious now that she had all the puzzle pieces. She was not absorbing his emotions. And now that she thought about it, she also didn't notice any emotions other than her own while in the Aniimarus company.

Celia hurried to catch up to his side. "Hey, Rees?"

"Yes?"

"How do you know so much?" She tilted her head, looking at him expectantly, but he kept moving forward. Celia spoke again. "I mean you seem to have all the answers, but every time I ask you how, you avoid the question."

When he still did not answer, Celia reached for his arm but stopped herself when she remembered that he didn't like physical contact without permission. So instead, knowing he could read her mind, she envisioned yanking on his arm and forcing him to look at her.

He shook his head. "Was that really necessary?"

Celia hurried to walk in front of him with her arms crossed forcing him to stop and stared him down. "Yes, it is necessary when you won't give me a straight answer."

Rees shot her a mischievous smile. "You have a lot of anger."

Celia guffawed. "No. I have a lot of frustration. You try having a straightforward conversation with yourself and see how you like it. You're not exactly easy to talk to."

Rees grinned. "We must keep up with the others, they won't wait for us and it'll be harder to get past the force field without them."

Celia's eyes widened in terror. "Force field?"

He didn't answer and Brody, Carl, and Lucy were catching up to them.

Carl arrived first, breathing heavy. He bent over, his peach fuzz blonde hair was so fair he appeared almost bald in the hot sunlight. His bright blue eyes looked pleadingly, as he talked through gasps with his hands on his knees. "What's the hold-up? Group meeting?"

Lucy, with her pixie cut purple hair and wide dark green eyes stopped next to him and laughed. "You gonna be okay, Carl? Not used to all this walking, eh?"

Carl stood up straight and glared at her. "Oh, shut it, Lucy. You try being as short as I am and keeping up with all you giants!"

Brody got to them last but did not stop. His muscular build appeared smaller than normal from slouching as he walked, such a stark contrast from his typical proud and head-held high demeanor. He kept moving past them as he spoke. "Come on everyone, stay together." He spared Celia a shy glance as he passed by her.

"Come on, troops! Let's get a move on!" Lucy grinned ear to ear as she jogged backward before turning around and following behind Brody.

Carl rolled his eyes and fake cried as he trudged forwards.

Celia hung back with Rees a moment before the two also followed, walking in sync. She spoke quietly so only he could hear. "Since you seem to know everything... Do you really think now is the right time to be going to the Capitol? I mean, I really think the more important problem is dealing with the coming attack from the evil souls."

Rees looked at her sideways before speaking through his telepathy. "I am only here because you asked me to be. The choices you make are yours."

Celia narrowed her gray eyes at him as irritation flared within her. "Seriously Rees, I'm asking for your opinion. Humor me."

He glanced at her with a resigned look on his face before he spoke. "I'm sorry. I have not seen my father since I was a child. I am apprehensive."

Celia tried to imagine being estranged from her family. The Aniimarus were kind, but they weren't even the same species as Rees. She had not given it much thought, but she realized now how much there was of him, and his life to get to know.

Her empathy and patience grew for him. She sent him mental images of holding his hand and then smiled at him. "I'm sorry Rees. I've kind of blown into your life huh?"

He returned her smile. "Technically I've pulled you into mine." He winked. "I could have just let things play out. But I intervened, I am responsible for you and your people."

Celia's heart sank a little at the idea of just being a responsibility to him, but tried to hide her thoughts and continued to listen.

"You are making the right choice. We need good relations with the Capitol if we are to get access to healing ponds. That is where we will find the butipods to grow the cinis plants around the Sanctuary boundary."

Celia felt the flutter of panic that dwindling time can cause. "Do we have enough time for all of this? Cultivating relations, finding the butipods, and once we have that how long will they take to grow? Can't we just get more pollen from the Aniimarus village?"

Rees patted Celia's back and warmth spread from where he touched her before he said. "Please calm. We have time."

She was getting tired of his placating nature. Then it dawned on her that even though he appeared close in age to her, she really did not know. Maybe he was interacting with her in such a way because he was actually much older. She was about to ask him when he spoke with his telepathy.

"I was five Earth years old when your people arrived on Meraiis. And I am not placating you. I am trying to comfort you. Sometimes things get lost in translation." He took a breath and looked at her. "You are not just a responsibility to me, even though it is true, I do not want to ever see any harm come to you."

Heat blossomed in her cheeks, and she was grateful that her long curly hair was down to hide the blush. "So how much further is the Capitol?" After days of back-to-back traveling on foot, her legs were burning and her feet felt like one more step would ignite them on fire then crumble the bones down to ash.

Rees smiled. "Don't worry, you will not burn. We are only a few more yards away from the travel tubes."

Celia wanted to playfully punch his arm in response to his chuckle, but she refrained.

A few minutes later they finally came to the end of the pale red field. She could no longer see her home's border behind her. The various shades of dark red forest before them sent a chill up her spine as towering trees blocked out the sun.

Celia cautiously walked forward following in Rees's footsteps when he suddenly sidestepped and took long strides away from her.

"Brody would like to speak with you."

She hated that her skin crawled from the idea of talking with him. Brody was her best friend and she worried that they would never be able to get back to where they used to be with each other.

A few feet ahead she saw him hanging back to wait for her. Her footsteps grew heavy and she avoided eye contact as he spoke. "Hey."

"Hey."

He gently brushed her elbow. "Will you please look at me?"

Celia cringed at his touch and planted her feet firmly before reluctantly looking at him with a glare in her eye. "What do you want, Brody?"

He played with the dirt at his feet with his hands in his pockets. "I know why you're mad at me. I didn't remember right away when Carl and Lucy found me. But then it slowly started coming back." His pleading eyes finally made contact with hers. "Please, Celia. You're my best friend. You have to know that wasn't me. I wouldn't ever treat you like that, let alone try to hurt you." He softly reached for her hand, but Celia crossed her arm as he continued to speak. "Please. I'm so sorry. I can't lose you, Celia. You mean everything to me."

Celia swiped away at the involuntary tear that fell down her cheek. "Just give me some space and time okay?"

Brody nodded his head as he turned and walked away. Celia sniffled and wiped her nose on her sleeve. She looked to the side and saw Rees watching.

"The travel tubes are just ahead. They are waiting for us."

Celia could hear what seemed like a bubbling brook, but thicker, like sludge ready and waiting to suck them into its tar. She moved a red branch out the way and before her on the forest floor were a dozen streams of heavy flowing water, like skinny rivers of thick blood in the ground.

The last of the Meraiin soldiers, with the exception of Alva, stepped into their own stream and lay down. The blood waters wrapped around them like living waves trapping their prey and they sank and disappeared.

Lucy gasped in terror and Carl hung onto her from behind shaking at the knees. "I am not getting in that!" She shrieked.

Brody approached Rees for the first time and Celia tensed in apprehension.

"Hey man, I want to thank you for saving Celia." Brody said.

Celia could not hear Rees's response, but Brody laughed and said. "Yeah, she is."

Brody patted Rees on the back and Rees did not cringe away but put his arm around Brody's neck and laughed.

Celia's mind was reeling. What the fuck?

Rees looked back at her and smiled. He then stood facing their group. The rest of the Meraiin soldiers had gone and Alva stood impatiently tapping a toe with her strong pearlescent arms crossed, her bright orange eyes flared with irritation.

Celia assumed Rees was speaking with them all telepathically at the same time as they were all looking at him with intent.

"These waters are not made of blood. They are safe. You simply lay down into a stream and it will transport you to the Capitol."

Lucy still had a bit of shrillness to her voice as she spoke. "I don't feel like drowning today, buddy. Think I'll take the long way."

"This would be impossible. There is a force field around the Capitol, these streams are the only way in or out and they are guarded."

For the first time, Celia looked around and saw the herd of deer watching and waiting for any of them to take a wrong step. The fine hairs on Celia's arms and neck stood on end. She shook off the feeling and announced to the rest. "I'll go first."

"Just walk in and lay down."

Celia nodded, then slowly took each step forward until the flowing thick blood–like water swallowed her feet. She was surprised to find that she did not feel wetness seep into her shoes. She carefully sat, then laid down into the stream. The water wrapped itself around her and she held her breath expecting it to flood in through her nose, mouth, and hair, but instead, it was as though she were wrapped inside a tube. All she could see was glowing red and hear the echo of her breathing.

Nothing happened right away, and her pulse quickened as she imagined herself being trapped forever and suffocating. She tried to sit back up but was held in place by an invisible force. A sulfurous scent flooded her nostrils, and a loud buzzing sound vibrated her body. She clenched her teeth as the noise increased and she squeezed her eyes shut.

Suddenly, it was as though a great force built up from her toes to the tip of her forehead and she was pushed forward by an overpowering wind. The air pressed in on her as she wound her way through underground tubes. She screamed out and just when she thought it might never end, the pressure eased, silence returned, and blackness surrounded her.

Chapter Twelve

The blood waves slowly parted from in front of Celia's vision to allow light in. Despite having the ability to breathe the entire journey within the tube, she sat up gasping for fresh and open air. If she never had to go in those tubes again, she'd be happy. Her skin quivered as though she were wearing a suit made of thousands of tiny invisible bugs. She sat up and scrambled out, digging her fingernails in the dirt on either side of the red river that left no wetness, to push herself up. She shook her arms out trying to rid herself of the unsettling feeling as the other streams opened to reveal her friends.

Lucy jumped out screaming. "Get them off! Get them the frick off of me!" She was frantically brushing her arms and legs.

Celia hurried over to her and placed her hands on Lucy's shoulders. "Lucy! Lucy, there's nothing there, look. It's okay."

Lucy's breathing slowed as she looked all over her body as best she could to find not a single moving thing was on her.

Carl climbed out of his tube looking very pale, "I think I might be sick." he said as he bent over with his hands on his knees.

Brody got out last. He had the same nauseated and unsettled appearance, yet he tried the hardest to save face by hiding his emotions.

Rees stood last, taking his time to rise. "It helps if you don't get up so quickly." He said to them all.

Celia glared at him. "You could have warned us, Rees."

Rees stared at her a moment before he stoically turned around to point ahead. "The Capitol is just through the brush here." This time he spoke his melodic language out loud while translating in their minds.

Celia fluttered within from the memory of the first time he whispered his words to her. It was such a beautiful language. She couldn't imagine ever getting used to the gentle melodic flow of the tinkling with soft chimes that rose and fell.

He continued to speak out loud while translating. "It is considered treasonous to speak another language within the Capitol territory. So please do not speak your Earth tongue within Meraiin presence while you are here."

Celia didn't think it was possible, but Carl dropped to an even lighter shade of pale, almost ghostly. She went to him and gently placed a hand on his arm. "Are you okay?"

He silently stared into a great nothingness before he whispered to her. "The Sanctuary hasn't seen any violence in over fifteen years. Basically since I was a toddler. The only soldiers that get any actual real training, are the ones who work directly for your parents, like Brody. The perimeter soldiers are basically glorified guard dogs, low maintenance you know? Lucy does extra work outs on her own, I don't know, because she's a glutton for punishment." He shrugged his shoulders. "I don't think I'm ready for this."

Celia dropped her hands and looked at him reassuringly. "I'm not expecting any fighting here either, Carl. I don't know Meraiin protocol, and I don't know if it would be safe to send you back on your own. Besides, we've come this far already, right?" Celia took a deep breath and let it out slowly. "Just come with us to the Capitol, it'll be an adventure! Think of all the new things we'll be able to see and do. Besides, I could use all the friends I can get."

She flashed him a winning grin and Carl reluctantly nodded his head. The uncertainty of their journey to come gnawed on the edge of Celia's mind. What if she was sending Carl and the others into danger? She was responsible, not just for the success of their mission, but for her friend's safety as well. They had their own lives with people waiting for them back at the Sanctuary, and it was on her shoulders to bring them home safely. The heaviness of having another person's life hanging on her consciousness was overwhelming.

Celia startled when Rees spoke to her mind. "Your fears are not unfounded, but it is unlikely that we are walking into death sentences. I will do my best to alert you to any danger. For now, please ensure that your friends do not speak in front of any Meraiin." He turned and looked at her pointedly. "Also, you need to calm Brody down. The sensation of the tubes and his recent possession have him on edge, he's ready to fight anyone who gives him the slightest reason, it will not end well for him."

At that Rees turned away and started to walk through the light red brush following after Alva. Celia spoke to her friends quickly and quietly. "Listen. You all heard Rees earlier right?" Brody, Carl, and Lucy silently nodded. "Well, it's really important that you take him seriously. Please don't talk in front of any Meraiin. We don't need to give them any reason to attack."

Brody scoffed. "I'm ready. Someone slips up, I'll show them what they're dealing with."

Celia shot him a glare. "I mean it, Brody. You have to keep your cool here. We don't know what we're dealing with."

Brody crossed his arms, voice threatening. "They don't know what they're dealing with."

Irritation and frustration radiated through Celia's body. "Seriously, Brody? What is your problem? Are you going to throw fireballs at anyone who looks at you wrong? Punch down anything that stands in your way? We have a chance here to make some real progress for our people's future. Your powers and super strength are not the solution to every problem." She stared him down. "You should know that better than most." Finally, he relaxed his arms and averted his gaze.

Carl and Lucy both looked at them uncomfortably until Lucy cut the silence. "You got it boss lady. No talking." She smiled and waved them all to move on. "Come on, let's get this show on the road, shall we?" She walked forward and everyone started to follow.

Just then, Rees's voice bellowed in Celia's head from afar and she stopped suddenly. "Wait!" Celia shouted at her friends. They all stopped and stared, waiting patiently. Then Celia listened to Rees.

"They need to leave their weapons here. Anything they have. Guns, knives, anything else that could be misconstrued as a threat."

Celia nodded to herself then addressed everyone. "We need to leave our weapons here."

Carl blanched, Lucy wobbled, and Brody huffed and shouted. "No fucking way! I'm not leaving my protection behind."

Celia scoffed at him. "Oh really? But a second ago you were touting around your strength, are you suddenly weak without a gun, Brody?"

"Whatever, Celia." Brody shrugged off the rifle strapped to his chest.

Celia cleared away some plants at a spot next to a nearby tree. "We'll put all our weapons here and cover them up. We'll pick them up on our way back home." She wondered how long that might be and shuddered at the thought of not knowing when, or if she'd see her family again, but kept a brave face for the sake of her friends.

With everything hidden as best as they were able, Celia, following Rees, led her soldiers through brush. She parted the tall, wine colored grass, and finally, came to a clearing. Yards away across an open field, stood a sight she never could have imagined.

Where the Aniimarus village was various shades of blue with the exception of the colorful Paliios, the Meraiin Capitolwas varying shades of red but mostly dark where the Aniimarus village was light. As though, with the Aniimarus the sunslight was welcomed, and here at the Meraiin Capitol, it was shut out. Similar to the Aniimarus village, the city was built from plant life. Trees and vines that grew tall into the forms of pointed skyscrapers at the town's heart and short stout huts instead of small alcoves around the perimeter.

But this city was at least a dozen times the size of the modest Aniimarus village, and this town moved. It flowed and shimmered like a mirage, as if she were to blink long enough, it would disappear from sight. Or perhaps its movement was the act of devouring, trapping its residents within its growing cells and eating them whole.

It was unsettlingly quiet. Celia felt eyes on the back of her neck and her skin crawled. She looked around but did not see anyone else other than Rees, and Alva a little way ahead waiting for them. Something about this place was wrong. Celia's every fine arm hair stood on end, as if something was watching them, waiting.

She felt a tug on her arm and Celia looked to her side. Lucy stared at her with pleading eyes, as if saying, 'We aren't seriously going in there, are we?'. Celia was silent and gave Lucy's arm a gentle squeeze then walked forward.

Chapter Thirteen

Rees tried, but failed to block the humans energy as they walked into town. Their celestial waves were powerful. Their silver threads, invisible to their eyes, that connected them to the universe thickened and vibrated with their increased anticipation. Rees exerted additional effort trying not to look into their waves to see the thoughts that simmered there. They were all the same anyway, filled with fear of the unknown. Of course, Celia's thoughts were always the strongest. From the moment she was born it was as though her waves, her essence, reached out to him, impossible to ignore even from so many solar systems away.

He did find it interesting that their human eyes could not see every aspect of the Capitol. To them, it danced and shimmered. For him it was solid. A pulsating powerful living thing. Their human eyes could not see the full spectrum of the colors surrounding them. Where they saw shades of crimson, wine, and pink, he saw it all. Including the infrared and ultraviolet images. The heat spots, the dark pockets of glowing and humming black bioluminescent ooze. Covering it all were the ever-constant fast-moving silver streams connecting all living things, plants, animals, and people alike and within those streams their consciousness.

The whole Capitol already knew he was home. No matter if he hadn't stepped foot in the territory since he was five years old, his species never forgot. He missed the Aniimarus village, his home. So many angry thoughts were being flowed in his direction here, it was hard not to drown in them. He mentally reached out for Celia. Her comforting warm waves were always a reassurance. The feel of her soul the most clear, her thoughts the loudest, even if having conversation in her language, in her mind, was something to get used to, it was worth the effort to know her, to feel her.

"Pinning for a human, Redreesishual?" Alva mocked him.

He shrugged her off. At least the rest of the army had returned to the Capitol at normal speed. Only Alva remained behind to follow him and the earthlings at their much slower human pace. Rees knew what waited inside the city center. The Meraiin, always in such a rush, not taking the time to see the things around them. If only they could appreciate how far their reach was, how many civilizations they could help, but no, their belief that they should never intervene held them in their place of opulence, watching and judging.

The closer they got to the city, the more streams that found their way to him. He wasn't used to blocking so many celestial waves. Their silver streams a massive tangle surrounding him as he walked. A handful jumped out the strongest. Among them, Dairea, his betrothed assigned at birth, and Fridiias, his father the king.

Dairea had hopeful visions of his return that Rees tried to shrug off. He tried not to think of Celia for fear of Dairea noticing how much he cared for his girl from Earth. Dairea was not going to welcome her, even Meraiin had jealous tendencies that could manifest in violent ways. But he welcomed Dairea's hopefulness, over Fridiias's thoughts that turned his stomach sour and his blood cold.

"Come on earth lover, pick up the pace, we're losing daylight." Alva sneered at him, her sharp teeth as white and pearlescent as her skin, and throwing a celestial wave his direction that was as flammable as her vivid orange hair and eyes.

They at last approached the black tar moat that surrounded the Capitol, and he had to hold out an arm to stop Celia from walking into it. Apparently the humans could not see the danger that lay in front of them. They all stopped and looked at him, while he looked at the ruby vines that were growing down towards them to form a bridge.

When the vines were done forming, Rees followed Alva and led them across. He could see Celia's alarm amp up and she asked him telepathically if she could hold his hand. His heart thumped from the desire to say yes. To feel her palm against his, warm and tight, but his trepidation at making her an even bigger target because of such a simple thing overruled his want. He shook his head no, and he could see the sadness in her eyes that almost broke him of his resolve.

Inside, the Capitol was humming with life. A massive single tower that reached towards the stars, filled with crisscrossing staircases and corridors made of the crimson vines. The Meraiin going about their hectic lives, all dressed in different colors of dark robes, paused long enough to stare or glare at him as they passed Rees by. As they neared a large open lobby that served as one of many meeting places, Dairea appeared, dressed in a deep purple full body-suit and a black cape. She was waiting for them, for him.

Dairea had the same dark iridescent skin and violet eyes as Rees. Her lithe frame shrouded in cascades of black hair, fit perfectly against Rees's body as she enveloped herself against him. Rees wanted to push her away, but he feared her wrath and retribution against Celia if he were to turn her back. And in this place filled with Meraiin who hated him, he needed any help he could get, even if Dairea had her own agenda.

Rees could see the heartbreak and betrayal fill Celia's thoughts just before she tried to shut him out of her mind. He wanted to tell her that it wasn't what she thought, but he couldn't, not without Dairea hearing as well.

Rees watched as Celia hugged herself and Brody wrapped an arm around her shoulders and kissed the top of her head, and when Celia leaned into Brody, it was as though Rees's heart was being squeezed tight. At the same time he was grateful to Brody and his protective nature over Celia. Even if she did not feel the same way about Brody as he did for her, Rees knew that Brody would stand by Celia's side when Rees could not.

Dairea stepped back keeping hold of Rees's arms as she looked at him and smiled. "Redreesishual! Oh how I've missed you." She peeked behind him. "And I see you've brought some friends." She released his arm and turned to walk away talking to him as she went. "Come, your father will want to see you."

Rees's skin crawled where Dairea had held him and he tried to force a smile.

"I'll leave them in your care." Alva said and gave a small bow to Dairea.

"Thank you, Alva." Dairea smiled. Alva turned on a heel and left them.

Rees followed Dairea to a nearby large platform. The others came along behind them, and when they were all within the circle, vines grew around them like a large cage and began to crawl up the wall. He sensed Lucy's thoughts, and just as she was about to let out an explicative, he spoke to her mind, a reminder to be silent.

Lucy nodded to him and Rees saw the question in Carl's thoughts, but he stayed quiet. Nervous energy was devouring Rees. It was going to be harder than he thought to protect his new friends. When the vine cage stopped crawling, the living wall before them parted to reveal a long, tall, and narrow hallway.

Rees forced himself to place his other hand on top of Dairea's when she tucked an arm through his. He despised how she so easily disregarded his personal space, but being his betrothed at birth, the societal rules did not apply.

Besides a united front would be best when they greeted Fridiias.

When they reached the end of the hallway the solid wall in front of them started to part. It grew slowly until it was wide enough to allow their party to enter. Before them, the massive open throne room with its web of seats surrounding the outer spaces, like the inside of a blood red beehive. It was filled with all the Meraiin of power, hundreds of them.

Rees's pulse raced as he looked around at them all and their angry silver celestial waves directed at him. At the center, sat Fridiias. The largest and strongest Meraiin in the room. A crown a thorns atop his dark iridescent hairless skin. His violet eyes fuming, and a frown across his vexed face.

Rees shivered with alarm and held Dairea's arm tighter.

Fridiias stood from his throne, his black robes flowing behind him as he stalked toward him. Rees forced himself not to cower. Forcing himself to make eye contact with his father.

Fridiias towered over him and glared. "How dare you return here, and with them." Rees felt the sting of the slap before he saw it coming. The imprint of Fridiias's hand across his face flushed with heat. His father's voice boomed above the hum of voices spreading throughout the hive. "The penalty for a banished returned without welcome, is death."

Chapter Fourteen

Rees's stomach twisted and turned with fear and dread as the guards with pearlescent skin around the perimeter of the room started to close in on him. The tips of his fingers and toes turned cold as he froze in terror. Fridiias turned his back on him, seemingly so he wouldn't have to watch the death of his son. Then Dairea spoke, halting the guards in place and forcing Fridiias to look back at her.

"All knowing, with honor I remind you that Redreesishual is my betrothed, and has been of age for many moons now, as such, I welcome him."

Surprise twisted Fridiias's face with shocked silence before he gathered his composure and addressed Dairea. "You would consummate your bond to allow him to stay?"

Dairea clasped her hands and held her head high. "Given the circumstances of his banishment, and to avoid an unnecessary death," she said pointedly, "I propose a surrogate."

Alarmed chatter echoed throughout the hive in hushed tones. Rees's dread eased away as hope took its place.

Fridiias stood in the center of the room, his chest rising and falling rapidly before speaking. "We have not had a successful surrogate in over fifty lifetimes. What makes you believe yours would be successful?"

Dairea spoke calmly yet confidently. "Redreesishual has found his soulmate, I believe he is in love with this human girl."

She gestured to Celia and Rees's instinct to protect her kicked into overdrive. He swiftly placed himself in front of Celia, reaching behind him to shield her from the view of his father.

He saw Celia and her friend's become alert to his reaction and a possible attack and Celia spoke to him in her mind. "Rees, please tell me what's happening?"

"An attempt to overthrow power. Please stay still." He then saw Brody's thought to shoot a fireball at Fridiias and Rees shouted into all of their minds. "No sudden movements or we all die. Trust me, Brody."

Rees could see the fear of the unknown creep back into all of the human's minds and they stilled, waiting for whatever might come next.

Rees anxiously waited while the chatter around the room intensified. Then Dairea spoke again. "All Knowing, this has been forthcoming since the moment you banished your son. It is the only way to successfully maintain The Origin."

Rees's stomach clenched as his father's body shook in angry defeat. If Fridiias had successfully killed Rees, The Origin would have transferred back to his father, and Fridiias, without a living wife, could have started anew. But the greatest Meraiin sin is unnecessarily killing your child, and Dairea made it unnecessary when she welcomed Rees back. While Rees knew his father would kill him anyway, Fridiias would not openly do so in front of so many powerful Meraiin. To the hive, it appeared that Dairea had found the only nonviolent solution to the succession of power.

She won.

Fridiias's shoulders dropped and hate flashed in his eyes. "Who is your surrogate?"

"Tiimas, your all knowing." Dairea said.

"Very well." Fridiias addressed the entire chamber. "As we all know, a time must come when The Origin must find a new line. For the first time in over fifty lifetimes, a surrogacy will take the transfer of power. It will be done after the next moon cycle. Let it be known, Dairea of the Cautiisian line will be mother of The Origin, and Tiimas of line Duiistian will be father. And so it is."

"AND SO IT IS." The words were repeated as one, by all the Meraiin within the massive chamber. Hundreds of voices echoed through their mouths like a loud buzz from where they were seated in their blood-red honeycombs.

The solid walls began to part, and the Meraiin in the massive chamber started to exit out of the openings behind their seats. Rees watched Dairea as she turned to face him and the humans with a smile plastered on her face like a cat with a belly full of warm milk.

"Well, I don't believe that could have gone better, do you?" She asked rhetorically.

Rees's muscles, taught with adrenaline, tried to keep his voice calm. "That was a huge risk Dairea. I'll have a target on my back until the transfer can take place." He paused and scoffed. "But you knew that already and took a chance anyway."

Dairea glared at him. "You caused this, Redreesishual, the moment you made the choice that you did all those years ago." She snapped at him. "Did you expect I would go about my life quietly?"

He squinted his eyes and shook his head. "I wasn't thinking about such things back then, and you weren't either Dairea, we were children. I was just doing what I thought was right."

Dairea crossed her arms, head tilted and feet planted. "Are you saying you dislike the outcome?"

Rees thought for a moment and let out a deep breath slowly. "No. I don't dislike it, but I also would like to keep living."

Dairea smiled sweetly and looped her arm through his. "Perfect. Just you wait and see, this month will go by quicker than you realize." She started to walk towards the exit. "Tiimas has one of the largest hives in the colony. Of course he'll be just as motivated to keep you alive, and I'm sure he'd be happy to host your guests as well." She smiled and nodded at the group of humans following them.

Rees could not deny that if he lived through the month, the idea of a fresh start had its appeal. But his friends' lives were at risk as well, and he didn't know if he could handle the loss of any one of them, especially Celia.

Celia's gentle yet alarmed, and familiar voice entered his mind. "Rees, what's happening? Where are we going?"

How could he explain it all? That her soul had called out to him the moment she was born. That he gave up his family, his home, just so she would have a chance to live. That he'd watched over her, her whole life. That she meant everything to him. That she was his whole universe.

Even though he knew she had an attraction to him, and he felt her energy reaching for his. She didn't know the full extent of his feelings. She was in the dark. He noticed her jealousy when Dairea embraced him. He wanted to explain. He wanted to tell her everything. But so much had just transpired in the throne room, it was impossible to go into the details right now about the politics of Meraiis, let alone his feelings for her.

How could he explain the depth of connection that there was within all living things in the universe, and that despite this universal connection between all living things, their connection, his and Celia's was even stronger, and that his possession of The Origin allowed him to see these connections. Their souls were meant to be together. How could any person understand so much in such a short time.

He was scared she'd run away from him.

He couldn't lose her.

She stared at him, waiting for an answer. He averted his eyes and said. "We are going to a friends." That was all he could bring himself to say.

He saw the flutter of irritation in her eye and he knew she was tiring of his short answers, but how could he tell her that they all just barely escaped death and were now going to be forced to stay here for one month's time?

He knew, or at least hoped, since the evil souls seemed to be gaining in strength, that they had a minimum of five weeks before the evil souls would be strong enough to mount another attack due to the detailed oral history his Aniimarus family kept of the war. But would they make it in time after traveling to the healing ponds?

He was naive to think that they had a chance of explaining the Sanctuary threat to his father, and Rees's hope was misplaced to think Fridiias would then let them simply pass through the Capitol territory. But here they were, and the outcome had a chance of success, if only they could avoid the threat of execution.

So lost in his thoughts Rees was surprised when they arrived so quickly at Tiimas's hive. The pulsating thick scarlet walls glowed pink alerting the owner to their arrival. The wall before them grew a circle opening large enough for them all to walk through.

Tiimas greeted Dairea with open arms. "How did it go?"

"Splendidly!" She said. "Although we're going to have a few extra guests for a while." She wrapped herself in Tiimas's embrace and kissed him passionately.

Rees averted his eyes and cleared his throat. "We've had a long journey, Dairea."

Tiimas, dark iridescent skin, short cropped black hair, and violet eyes, was dressed in a black suit instead of the typical robes. He broke their kiss and grinned in a way that did not reach his eyes. "You must be Redreesishual, welcome to my home." He said as Dairea stood by Tiimas's side with an arm around his waist.

Rees reached out, and the two shook hands. "Thank you for hosting us."

"Of course!" He said with an enthusiastic flair and that same fake smile. "Let me show you to your rooms."

As they walked through Tiimas's home, Rees could see the thoughts swirling in his friends' heads, ready to explode with questions.

Tiimas stopped in front of a wall and gestured towards it. "You and your friends can have this wing to yourself. There's three rooms, so some will have to share. I'll have my help bring you some nourishment." The crimson wall opened. "Enjoy your stay."

Tiimas and Dairea walked away, and Rees and the humans entered the room. It was large enough to have a seating space, dining room, and three hallways that no doubt led to the three sleep and cleanse chambers.

A pale pink pillow big enough for ten people to sit on was in the center of the room. Rees stumbled towards it, exhausted, he fell into its cushion face first.

In moments he was falling into sleep when he was shaken roughly by Brody. "Yo! Alien, you've got some fucking explaining to do!"

Rees groaned and rolled over, still laying down but facing them. He started to speak out loud and all he saw was confusion on their faces. He was so tired he forgot to translate in their minds, so he started again.

"Conscious thought presents as silver strands connecting all around the universe, we call this, Celestial Waves. The Origin is the very first conscious thought, the first strand. It has been passed down within Meraiin leadership since the beginning of time, it currently resides within me."

The humans all gasped, except for Brody, who scoffed. Celia's eyes widened, placed a hand across her mouth, and stood in stunned silence.

Rees continued. "Meraiin in power are assigned reproductive partners at birth, like your concept of marriage. When the ruling couple's first child is born, The Origin is transferred into that child. The only way to revert the line of succession is if that child dies, or willingly relinquishes The Origin. Most often, the child may say they want to relinquish, but subconsciously they don't want to let it go. If they are even minutely hesitant, removing The Origin kills them."

Brody rolled his eyes. "This is a great history lesson Rees even if it is true, but what does this have to do with what just happened back there? They looked like they wanted to kill Celia."

Rees took a deep breath and sat up rubbing his temples. "Dairea, as my assigned betrothed, is harder to block my thoughts from. She saw that I have... a connection, with Celia. If a carrier of the origin procreates with someone other than his or her betrothed, it is believed that The Origin can become... tainted. It's believed the Origin would be tainted, like your idea of turning evil, like devils or human possession. Although, that is not something that I believe, and it has never been proven. But they would have killed her to prevent that risk."

Rees looked at Brody who was distinctly a shade greener than a second ago, but didn't say anything. Celia's cheeks paled and her hand dropped from her mouth to run her fingers nervously through her hair.

Rees continued. "Dairea proposed a surrogacy. It is a transfer of The Origin from one Meraiin to another. In one month time, I will give The Origin to Tiimas. However, my father will be waiting for any opportunity to stop the change in the line of succession. He will try to kill me in order to have The Origin transferred back to himself before Tiimas takes over. And my father has many supporters who will be on his side."

Rees looked up to see Celia throwing him a furious look, with a wildness in her eyes. "One month! What is the Sanctuary supposed to do for one month, Rees? Pray they don't get taken over and demolished by evil souls?" She did not wait for him to answer. Her voice went up a notch in pitch. "We don't have time for this royalty bullshit, Rees! Why are we here? I trusted you to help us!"

Her words hurt Rees more than he wanted to admit. He watched Lucy place a hand on Celia's shoulder, her voice calm and placating. "Celia, hun, Rees just told us that he basically has a hit out on him by his own father. Maybe ease up a bit? I'm pretty sure he did everything he could to help us. We'll just have to go back on our own and figure it out."

Rees shook his head. "It's not safe for you to leave until the transfer is complete. The souls won't be strong enough to mount an attack for at least five weeks, we know this from experience during the Beast Wars, they work together as one and need time to recharge after an attack, Brody's possession was no doubt an attack. The transfer is in four, that gives us one week to get to the healing ponds and back to the Sanctuary."

Celia stalked off down one of the hallways, arms crossed, and head shaking, with Brody following her. Rees tried to read her thoughts, but she was blocking him with every bit of effort she had. Did she not care about his life at all? Rees went down an opposite hallway and entered one of the sleeping chambers. He never should have intervened. He hated being back here. He missed his home, Oisin, Aoife, Padraig, and Darragh.

Even though Meraiin did not need as much sleep as earthlings, he was mentally drained from being around so many emotionally charged celestial waves, not to mention the turmoil he was just put through. He laid down on another small, yet still big enough for two adults, pink pillow and fell into a deep sleep.

Chapter Fifteen

The days waiting for safe exit out of the capitol passed by as one monotonous glob. Their tension and fear had a way of being muffled when they were safe, and extraordinarily bored, inside of Tiimas's hive. The Humans orbited around each other like repelling magnets inside a small space.

What was that Earth term?

Cabin fever.

In the living room, with its natural grown furniture, Lucy shouted at Carl after losing another game of Goiiang, but Carl shooed away her frustrations and laughed at her latest failed attempt. Goiiang, a Meraiin pastime similar to the humans' game of chess, was proving difficult for Lucy to figure out. The game of Goiiang included black obsidian pieces that attached to a crystal clear three dimensional star; the points of the star were interchangeable, and just as crucial as the obsidian pieces during game play. Rees had offered to explain the game, but according to Lucy, she 'enjoyed a challenge'.

In the kitchen area, Brody spent an unnecessary amount of time creating a too large sandwich, then swore and clenched the sides of his head when he dropped it on the floor. Rees debated telling Brody that unlike his flat solid square Earth bread, Meraiin paniiem was round and hollow on purpose, he wasn't supposed to try and flatten two pieces. Paniiem was intended to be cut open, and filled with innards; but then the veins in Brody's forehead stood out and his face flushed.

Rees looked away.

Nope, I want no part of that.

When he looked to the last corner of the room, he found pain again. Every time Celia caught Rees's eye, she turned the other way.

His heart ached.

If only he could speak with her, or listen to her thoughts to try and understand, but still, she made a tremendous effort to block his mind. He understood her worry, her need to get back to her family in time; but the lack of care she had shown for his impending filicide, it was destroying him.

If only his mother were alive to speak some sense into Fridiias, but more than that, if she were here to embrace Rees, to sing to him and tell him everything would be okay, then maybe all would righten itself in this world. His insides were cold, lonely, and he doubted the decision to ever get involved all those years ago when we decided to guide that one beautiful Earth soul to Meraiis.

Boy Redreesishual should have listened to his father and never broken the law by helping them.

But the pull Celia had on him, even back then, all those light years away, could not be ignored. Brighter than any other stream of consciousness, unknowingly, she called to him and him alone. He would never regret guiding her aunt Annabelle to his planet. Even if Celia never cared for him again, it was worth it; they-Earth, even a tiny piece of that world, was worth saving.

She was worth saving.

Showing Annabelle how to control her existence after death, showing her how to communicate with Elijah, and lastly, showing her the way to Meraiis, was the cause of Rees' banishment. Afterall, 'the Meraiin do not intervene'. But Rees believed that was an outdated way of thinking. What was the point of having the Origin, the ability to tap into conscious thoughts across the universe, if not to help others? To help make the cosmos a better place. It didn't matter what Rees believed, he was still shunned by his father, his mother executed by the council for trying to intervene.

Haunted, and homeless as a five-year-old. He never would have survived if not for his adopted family eventually finding him.

Perhaps more intelligent and self-aware than an Earth child, but a child all the same, and it was an agonizing journey of loneliness.

But over the last twenty years, Rees had scrounged together a small slice of self-forgiveness, of happiness, and stability with his Aniimarus family, and he missed them.

Celia's cold shoulder only made the desire to run away back to his home even stronger. Only, it was too late, the damage of his returning to the Capitol was done. Fridiias would stop at nothing to take back the Origin. He would not rest until his son was dead.

A dark shadow fell over Rees and he tried to shake it off, but it wouldn't leave. He realized then, the shadow was real, not figurative. He stood swiftly, trying to wipe away the dark. The humans startled, staring at him with confused faces.

Lucy looked at him. "Rees, what is it?"

"The shadow." He spoke to her mind. "Don't you see it? It's all over me!"

A veil of dry slime withered its way around Rees' body snaking up his back and wrapping around his throat. He struggled against it, but like a ghost, he could not touch it. Eye's wide, and pulse throbbing in his ears as the shadow squeezed tighter.

The front door of their section of Tiimas' massive hive, slid open with ferocity, and just as quick as the shadow had appeared, it vanished.

Profound confusion traveled through his mind, but as Rees clutched at his neck, relief spread through him when the air in his lungs filled with ease.

What in the the stars was that?

He had never known of an evil soul getting into the capitol, and had never known one to be able to do anything other than possess. It almost reminded him of a premonition, a warning. Something his adopted mother Aoife had spoken of. Only the Aniimarus elders knew of such things.

But he did know those warnings usually related to those that the seer loved, not the seer themselves. If that was a warning for what was to come for Celia, he would be on even higher alert. Even though she wanted nothing to do with him, or so it seemed, he couldn't turn his heart off as easily, he would protect Celia at all costs.

He didn't have time to share with the others, and wasn't sure they'd believe him anyway. Rees turned his attention back to the open door where Dairea stood. Her hair wild, and dark iridescent cheeks a shade warmer, she shouted in their minds. "They're coming! We must leave, now!"

The humans didn't react immediately, as if it took their minds a few extra seconds to process what she said.

"Move!" She shouted again.

Panic filled the room and they all hurried after Dairea, grabbing go bags as they rushed through the exit and left Tiimas's guest wing. They ran through the halls of Tiimas's hive and stopped when they reached the main doors of the grand home. Tiimas stood there waiting for them in his suit.

Rees cringed when he saw a robed servant with pearlescent skin next to him. She was overloaded with a giant bag on her back, like a pack mule, ready for the trek ahead, but miserable about it. Rees would never accept the class division within the Capitol. The shade of an individual's skin should never equate their worth. The iridescent, like himself, Tiimas, and Dairea holding positions of power; and the pearlescent holding positions of guard duty and servitude, was immoral.

Tiimas, not bothering to speak to the humans directly, spoke out loud in the Meraiin chime-like language, and Rees translated in their minds for the humans.

"Stay close, I have secured a way out of the Capitol for all of us, but should anyone stray, I will not rescue you, we will not wait. You will be imprisoned or worse should you get separated. Keep up."

Rees sensed a chill pass between the humans.

Outside Tiimas' hive, the red honeycomb-like halls were quiet, as if deserted on purpose. Tiimas must have paid handsomely to redirect the flow of foot traffic here, so that they could escape from Friidas soldiers undetected. They followed the Meraiin servant through the corridors, glancing behind their shoulders as they went.

After a few minutes of tense walking, they stopped at a dead end. Rees saw Brody clenching his fists and opened his mouth about to say something, but Rees turned to give him a warning look and shook his head. The servant bent down to where the floor met the wall, feeling for something unseen, until a downward hole opened near their feet. She sat and scooted her way into darkness.

The humans' thoughts all whirled in the same direction, fear of the unknown. Lucy's thoughts were the loudest.

"Nope, nope, nope." She spoke to herself in her head. "Okay Lucy, you got this, you can slide into the dark hole in the ground that goes who knows where and probably ends inside the mouth of some grotesque monster waiting for a meal. Yeah, sure, no big deal, you got this, girl!"

Despite the danger of the situation, Rees couldn't help but chuckle lightly as he watched Lucy shift her weight side to side as she pumped herself up. Tiimas and Dairea went first, followed by the humans, Celia, and then Rees went last.

The dark tunnel barely fit a full grown adult, the edges pressed against them as they made their way, like they were inside the intestines of the Capitol. Rees could feel the heat of Celia's body in front of him as they went. Their breathing, although heavy, was not heard, as though it was being absorbed, muffled, by the organic material of the tunnel.

They encountered a slick spot, perhaps where water had pooled, and Celia let the walls in her mind fall only momentarily.

He heard her thoughts. "Rees." A sound so full of mixed emotions, fear, desire, guilt. As if his name encompassed every feeling inside her, and was on repeat in her head. Rees craved her touch, he wanted to squeeze her hand, wanted to comfort her. But just as soon as her thoughts were glimpsed, she put her guard back up, and her mind was silent again.

Hope fluttered in his chest as sweat beaded his brow.

Rees heard the angry thoughts of Brody as Carl bumped into him when the servant, Tiimas, and Dairea stopped in front of them. Slowly, light filtered into the tunnel and they emerged into the forest that surrounded the Capitol.

The group stood, and stretched, everyone appeared relieved to be out and breathing fresh air. They continued their trek, following the servant through the thick underbrush, and winding through the trees, until they came to another blood river, a transportation tube, this one, on the opposite side of the Capitol.

Two guards stood on either side of the river, their collapsible swords drawn, and Rees' heart raced; but then calmed when Tiimas walked up to them, handed them each a pouch full of coins and shook their hands.

The two guards entered the travel tube first, then one at a time, their caravan entered the crimson stream and disappeared.

Chapter Sixteen

Darkness greeted Rees as he emerged from the Meraiis blood stream, the planet veins that ran through and around the world; but without light they appeared thick, dark, almost black. His dry skin tingled as he shook off the aftereffects of the travel tube. He squinted, looking for any sign of the others, difficult for him to see through the ever-present dark.

Rees struggled to understand, it wasn't like normal nightfall, it was as if he stood in the aftereffects of a forest fire. Blackened ash hung hazily in the air, so thick it blocked out the light. It hovered and occasionally sparked with golden flecks against the darkness, as if gravity had been displaced for only this ash. It shifted and flowed against his footsteps as he walked forward, like he was water and the ash was oil. It didn't stick but floated around any solid object.

There.

A handful of feet away, they stood in a circle. Tiimas broke off from the group and walked towards him.

Rees spoke in his tinkling Meraiin language to Tiimas. "Where are we?" He asked.

Tiimas stared incredulously. "The foothills of the healing territory. Does your beast family teach you nothing of our planet?"

Heat rushed up his neck, a flame of indignation mixed with slight awkward shame. Rees never did explore the entirety of the world. The Aniimarus taught him the ways of nature, showed him how to live with the planet, not against it, but there remained a distinct difference between hearing about a place and seeing it.

He never traveled much further than the Earth territory, the Capitol, and the Aniimarus village. In other words, the southeast section of the Meraiis planet. Perhaps, fear held him back. Because the Aniimarus were not allowed to travel too far outside of their village, Rees would have had to go on his own, and he never built up the courage to do so. Being disowned from his birth family at such a young age had a distinct effect on one's psyche in more ways than one.

He looked at Tiimas. "Why bring us here? That's the first place the Capitol soldiers will look, they knew of our plans to help the humans."

"Exactly, they will be coming here, but we have a head start. If we had waited, we wouldn't be able to get your humans what they need."

His eyes widened and a small sizzle traveled up his spine, head cocked to the side. "And that matters to you?"

Tiimas smiled. "Not particularly, but it matters to you."

Rees stood stock still, was Tiimas a decent soul? He hadn't imagined him as anything much more than an entitled power grabber, with his slicked back hair, and fitted suits.

"You know, Rees, I may not have as clear a line on your celestial waves, but I can still sense your reactions. Don't be so shocked. I'm not evil, like your father." He took a deep breath and looked to the black sky, not a single star shone, not even one of the moons could be seen. "To tell you the truth, I only agreed to Dairea's Origin transfer plan because your father had been leading our people down a path of selfishness, of evil. If there were a way for you to retain the Origin, and lead the people yourself... then I'd support that."

Rees heard, but could not believe, he narrowed his gaze. "Why would you support such a thing? Why support me, a traitor?"

Tiimas placed a large heavy hand on Rees' shoulder. "You and I both know, you are no traitor to the cause of goodness, only to your father's outdated rules."

Tiimas patted him on the back and returned to the group, speaking over his shoulder as he left. "Come on, Rees, let's save Earth, then ourselves."

A warmth blossomed within Rees as he walked with the others, hope. If Tiimas and Dairea really were on their side, then they had one less enemy to face. Perhaps Meraiis had a chance for a prosperous future. Maybe the class division between the pearlescent and iridescent could end. Perhaps the Aniimarus could integrate with the rest of the planet. Travel, learn, explore.

Then Rees looked at the servant. But then, why did Tiimas have an indentured? Something was off, something just out of sight, festering and waiting to emerge given the right opportunity. He lengthened his stride to catch up to the servant, knowing she wasn't supposed to speak directly to anyone unless spoken to first, and the last thing he wanted was to get her in trouble. But she was a living soul, and they were outside the Capitol.

He glanced at her sideways and spoke to her mind. "Hi."

No response, her cheeks pinked, her long white hair fell across her pearlescent skin, hiding her eyes.

"What's your name?" Rees asked.

She hesitated, and looked away, but responded in her mind. "Cerviias."

"Can I help carry some of that, Cerviias?"

She gave a slight shake of her head. "You're gonna get my pinky chopped."

Fear flooded his belly, he was putting her in danger just by being kind. It wasn't fair. It wasn't right. Tiimas hid something, no good soul could instill that type of fear within his own home.

"I apologize for my ignorance. Don't react, I'll walk a few paces ahead. But please, I hope you can help me." Rees sped up, walking at a short distance from the back of the group, and slightly in front of Cerviias. "Please, if you can tell me, what are their true intentions? Dairea and Tiimas."

"Sir, do not ask questions you are not ready to hear the answers to."

"Can we trust him?"

"I think you know already." She paused, but spoke again. "You can trust him to get the seeds you need, but your group must separate soon after, run if you have to."

His pulse throbbed in his ears, his neck hot. "Thank you for your honesty." He thought for a moment. "Come with us. When we leave, you can have a place in our group."

A strong wave of emotions flooded off Cerviias, he sensed her fear, shock, wanting, all mixed together before she quickly reigned it in, before her waves could reach the rest of the group.

"I will ensure your escape." She replied.

"Please, don't do that, don't risk yourself. Help us, by joining us." Rees pleaded earnestly.

"I'll try, sir." Her waves settled to a stoic calm once again. "Please, stay with your group sir."

Rees glanced quickly behind him and gave a small nod, then hurried to stay closer to the group. Out of habit he reached for the minds of the humans. Checking in on them one by one.

Lucy had her vivacity back, excited for the next step of their adventure. Scenes from books came to the forefront; pirates and sword fights played across her mind as they walked through the darkness.

Carl's mind, shrouded in fear, but determined to keep up, to not be left behind.

Brody, always on guard, always looking for the next threat, then drifting to thoughts of Celia as he stared at her backside.

Anger flushed up Rees's core, a strong urge to knock into Brody overcame him.

He elbowed Brody. "Apologies, I did not see you there." Rees spoke to his mind.

Brody huffed and rolled his shoulders, shaking his head.

Rees smiled on the inside, then stretched his telepathy for Celia. Silence. Still, so much silence from her, it tore him straight down the middle. Only her mind, the sound of her voice, her smile, could glue him back together.

When his feet fell in step with Dairea's, he asked her. "Why are the foothills so dark?"

She jolted slightly, surprised to have him next to her and talking out loud so suddenly. She seemed to consider his question before answering.

"As you know, the butipods reside in the healing ponds. When cultivated and planted they grow the Cinis plants, and their pollen-the Cinis dust, kills evil things; souls, infections, troubles of the mind, and so forth. But, if the butipods are left in the healing waters when the dying season comes, they split open in the water, releasing their inner Cinis pollen. It floods the waters.

"That's why the streams that run through this sector have such powerful healing properties. But when the ponds are full, saturated, the leftover Cinis rises to the surface and the wind blows its ash into the air. The mountains that surround this valley keep the dust trapped, like a giant fishbowl." She shrugged, and gestured around. "It's the dying season. We're surrounded by Cinis."

Rees's mouth hung open. It was so obvious now, why hadn't he realized. Of course he had learned of the planet's cycles, its seasons, but he never imagined the Cinis pollen would be trapped in a valley, its ash blocking out the sun for months at a time.

"How will we find the ponds? How do the guards know where to go? I can hardly see through the dust."

Dairea grinned at his worry. "Don't worry so much Rees, the guards know the path by heart, they are trained from birth to know these things, to be our guides and protectors."

And our slaves. Rees thought to himself, and hoped Dairea didn't pick up on the thought. If she did, she didn't react.

After a moment of continued walking with Dairea and silence, she spoke. "Tiimas bought us roughly one day's head start. If we get the butipods quick enough, we can rest here tonight, before we begin the journey up east mountain to the next transportation vein.

Rees nodded his understanding. They'd have to retrieve what they needed quickly. Then somehow, he'd have to get a message to the humans, and Cerviias, without alerting the attention of Dairea, Tiimas, and the two guards. He couldn't be certain that Dairea and Tiimas had nefarious intentions, but he trusted Cerviias and his instincts; and his instincts were screaming at him, they were headed to a trap.

They must escape tonight.

Chapter Seventeen

Their group continued forward as Rees's mind raced, not in panic, but in planning. Looking at each hypothetical scenario in his mind, turning it over and looking at it from every angle, taking it apart piece by piece and putting it back together. Seeing how each plan could succeed or fail. The safety of his friends relied on a successful escape and he couldn't bear it if one of them got hurt because of a faulty plan.

He had scarcely gotten all the pieces in place in his head when they arrived at the edge of an expansive smooth black surface. They gathered around, their faces lit by the occasional golden spark, sunlight piercing through small gaps in the Cinis ash and reflecting off its particles. The large black surface rippled as if caught in a breeze and Rees realized they stood next to a great lake, the healing ponds.

◻Tiimas gathered everyone's attention, speaking his language out loud while one of the guards translated in their minds for him.

◻"It's nearly nightfall."

Rees interrupted. "How can you tell?"

Tiimas turned to him. "My timekeeper." He said as if it were obvious, and pointed to a thin braided vine around his neck. At the end hung what looked like a tiny red rose. "It slowly opens and closes with the changing of the day."

Tiimas tried to hide his annoyance with a smile, but Rees could see his deceit behind the gesture, he could feel it too, in Tiimas's celestial waves.

Tiimas continued. "We have time for a short rest, then we need to get to work to retrieve the butipods. The goal is to harvest two of them, we won't have time to get more than that. We must not linger in this place, without a doubt the Capitol will be following us once they realize we're missing, we will depart first thing in the morning."

He nodded curtly and looked around before he continued to speak, leaving no space for debate. "We'll need a team of six, of course three of those will be the help." He said without skipping a beat and speaking for them.

Clearly it was second nature to him that Cerviias and the guards were only here to assist with his every whim rather than independent intellectual souls. "We'll need three more volunteers, I suggest the humans should choose amongst themselves seeing as the butipods are for their needs." He turned on a heel speaking over his shoulder.

"One shift, then we start the dive." Then he went to join Dairea a few paces away, who had set up a small picnic for only the two of them.

Carl anxiously walked up to Rees and asked in his mind. "What does one shift mean?"

"It's roughly the equivalent of your one Earth hour."

Carl nodded. "Thanks Rees!" and then ran off into the darkness.

Rees wondered what he was up to, and was concerned about him leaving the group by himself with no way to protect him. But he couldn't run after Carl and risk alerting Tiimas that he knew something was wrong. So instead, he did the only thing he could do. He walked around the edge of the pond, and as discreetly as he could, tugged at everyone's thoughts as he passed by them, gathering intel.

He had walked a good length of the pond, when he stopped short.

Rees sensed her before he saw her.

Celia no longer guarded her thoughts, believing that she was alone in the darkness of the ash. He felt the essence of her standing next to him. He heard a small sniffle.

Is she crying?

He listened to her mind race. "Why did I ask him to come to the Capitol? He could be at home, safe, with his Aniimarus family. It's all my fault he's going to die. How could a father treat his son like this?"

Heat blossomed in Rees' heart. So, she does care about me.

Warmth spread throughout his body, and he suddenly felt guilty for eavesdropping on her internal feelings. He stepped closer and saw the form of her body facing away from him. He slowly placed a hand on the small of her back.

She startled, and turned to look at him. "Rees."

His heart leapt at the sound of his name on her lips. She stood there, frozen, and staring at him. Mouth hanging open then closing shut at a loss for words. His arm had wrapped around her waist as she had turned, and he felt the muscles in her lower back twinge. He withdrew his touch quickly, realizing that he had not asked permission.

"I apologize-"

She cut him off. "I'm so sorry for the way I acted earlier." Her eyes pleaded with him to understand. She took a deep gulping breath and continued. "I was just so shocked at the way your father treated you, and mad, and scared."

"And guilty." She added in her head unintentionally. "And I took that out on you. And I am so sorry, Rees, I'm-"

Her words became soft, wobbly, and thick. He closed the small space between them.

Damn societal protocol.

He wrapped his arms around her, holding her tightly. She tucked her head underneath his chin and gripped his shirt between their chests as she cried into him, rocking their bodies with her sobs. He didn't know how to comfort her, and wished desperately to ease her pain, he did the only thing he could think of.

He sang Aoife's lullaby, softly in his tinkling language, whispering it to her as he ran his fingers through her curls and swayed them gently side to side.

The song spoke of the suns, the moons, and the stars. How every conscious thing flows through different planes, and at different times, and transforms and is reborn, but much like energy in motion, how it never ceases to be. It spoke of the colors of Meriias and how their ancestors had painted them onto the planet, mixing their magic into the pigments to create the different properties of each sector of the planet. It spoke of the strength of a wish, how willing a thing with your whole heart had power. And finally, it spoke of love, and truth, and kindness.

By the end of the song, Celia's tears had stopped and her clenched fists had relaxed against him.

Her breathing had steadied, and he spoke to her mind. "It's a lot to take in for anyone. You don't need to be sorry for a broken heart, I'll fix it for you."

She took a deep breath and shuddered as she released it. "Rees, you already did."

Her eyes sparkled, still wet with tears, but her soft lips curled up in a small smile. She smelled of vanilla, and goodness, and hope. He brushed a stray lock of hair behind her ear, he couldn't help himself.

Body shivering, he asked. "Can I kiss you?"

Answering with her body and not her words, she pressed her lips against his. A pleasant burn, like liquid cinnamon against skin, crept along his mouth, and he moved his lips with hers. She tasted of something sweet, and warm, and safe. He clung to her as if his life would stop without her. This human whose mind had spoken to him the moment she was born.

Her stardust was meant to meet with his.

She felt right in a way he could never explain.

They slowly parted and he could feel her heart racing beneath her shirt.

"Wow." A quiet laugh escaped her.

He smiled, vowing to never leave her side. "Yes indeed... wow." He nuzzled his nose against hers, savoring the moment, and breathing her in.

Chapter Eighteen

They stood in a small circle to better see each other, discussing next steps. The underwater village they were about to enter, the Aquafisiian territory, was a dangerous place. They did not appreciate outsiders stealing their natural resources, and they refused to negotiate any kind of trade.

Tiimas explained the harvest process and its dangers while one of the Guards translated in their minds, then he asked for participants. Rees watched in horror as Celia raised her arm high to volunteer, ash glowing around her with its golden sparks like a halo.

Every cell in his body screamed in alarm.

She's going to die.

You can't control her.

She'll resent you if you try to stop it.

Go with her, you'll protect her better by her side.

Rees raised his arm as well, while Brody and Lucy followed suit, shooting their hands up at the same time. Carl kept his hands clasped behind his back and looked anywhere but at the rest of them.

Tiimas laughed and spoke in his language. "Humans, so eager to die."

Rees narrowed his eyes, trying hard to keep his voice from turning sour. "Or they are brave. They aren't eager to die, they are eager to return home and save their people."

Tiimas looked like he wanted to laugh again, but stopped himself. Rees couldn't clearly identify his thoughts, but he could sense his wheels turning, changing direction fast.

Tiimas' expression switched from one of amusement to one of sincerity. "Of course, you're correct, I'm sorry friend. They have made an honorable gesture." He paused, looking around at the group of humans, and hesitated before saying. "It's still best if the guards and the servant are three of the six, they are stronger and more knowledgeable." He clapped Rees on the back and grinned before walking back towards Dairea. "I'll let you select the other three."

Rees shivered with unease. He couldn't tell Celia no, he would never be the person in her life trying to control her for his own desires. He must trust and support her decisions, no matter what they may be. Of course that meant he had to go with her. There was no way he'd ever let her walk into the fire on her own. That left one selection between Brody and Lucy. Brody's strength would be beneficial, but the retrieval process was delicate and Brody was quick to anger, he could end up letting his frustrations get the better of him, thereby sabotaging the mission.

Lucy seemed competent and levelheaded, but he'd also seen the fear in her mind, if she froze from terror, they could lose a butipod. Rees weighed the pros and cons and decided Brody had slightly more pros. Brody's strength and quickness to react, even if he shouldn't react so quickly in certain situations, would come in handy for this particular endeavor.

He nodded at each of them, and then spoke to their minds. "Thank you for your bravery, the Meriian guards and Cerviias," Rees paused to gesture to the woman standing behind him, "are very experienced and we are grateful for their service. Brody will join Celia and I to retrieve the butipods."

Lucy shifted her weight to one side and crossed her arms. "Oh come on! This is a once in a lifetime chance to see this place!"

"I understand." Rees telespoke. "But this situation isn't for sightseeing, it's dangerous, and we will most likely benefit from Brody's superstrength, I'm sorry Lucy."

Brody strutted like a peacock and Rees had the sudden urge to wipe the smugness off his face, but he reigned in his annoyance and focused on his breathing.

Lucy harrumphed and swung her arms as she walked away. Carl scurried after her, and Rees caught a glimpse of him whispering in her ear before they disappeared into the ash.

Rees turned to Celia. Her gray eyes reflected the golden sparks of the lake so clearly. Her curls had frizzed from so much travel and created a halo effect, highlighting the fierceness in her face but also her natural feminine beauty.

He was terrified of this being the last time he would see her.

"May I embrace you?" He asked her softly.

Celia's eyes held nothing but affection as she snuggled into his arms. Rees could hear Brody's surprised, jealous, and somewhat irritated thoughts coming from somewhere behind him, but he attempted to block Brody out and focus on Celia's quiet breathing against his chest.

"Please take heed to Tiimas' instructions, go slow, stay close." Rees murmured in her mind as he ran his hands across her arms and back. He couldn't risk also telling her to keep her guard up because he didn't trust Tiimas. He would have to be extra alert for the both of them.

The group of six walked close to the edge of the pond. Looking closely, small black bubbles rose up from the waters and popped slowly as if it were a tar pit and not smooth waters; another effect of the ash. Guard one, Whiisaas, stepped up to the bank and bent down to cup a bubble. He held it in his hands and instead of popping, it slowly expanded. When it was the right size, he lifted it above himself and slowly lowered it down on his head, then walked further out into the pond and dove in.

Rees' breathing ticked up a notch and his heart tapped his chest soft and fast. He reached for Celia's emotions and was surprised to find enchantment and excitement sitting there. She wasn't scared. He drew from her strength to find his own bravery and followed the others. The bubble forming in his hand and a slick sheen to it, like a layer of oil, slippery in his hold. He took his time, careful not to break it. When he lowered it over his head, it hardened with his first breath like a breathable helmet.

Something about the chemical composition of his exhale mixed with the interior of the bubble and he had an entirely closed breathing system around his head. The magic of this world continued to astound him. Perhaps Aoife had been right when she once, many moons ago, suggested that he spent too much time wrapped up in the minds of the people from Earth, and that he needed to explore his home planet more.

As soon as they sank beneath the surface of the water, it was as though someone turned on a dark golden light. He could see through the depths below much better than above. But the darkness still lingered. They swam, down, down, and down. The deeper they went, the brighter his surroundings became. Quite the opposite of what he had expected. Biolumences covered every hard surface. Glowing gray and golden light beams enveloped them.

Something in their surroundings shifted and suddenly his skin tingled. He reached for Celia's hand next to him and gripped tightly. Something was watching them.

Celia telespoke to him. "Rees, what's wrong? What did you see?"

"I do not know. There was a shadow. Slick, fast, small. But it gave me an uneasy feeling."

He watched as Celia seemed to speak to Brody with just her eyes. As though their shared childhood granted them their own unspoken language. She seemed to be telling him, 'eyes open'.

An unfamiliar emotion crept up Rees's back. He had an urge to put himself between Brody and Celia.

Jealousy?

Yes, that was it. He was jealous of their shared history. Rees wasn't sure why. He had been in Brody's mind and his affection for Celia was purely surface level. Physical attraction, awe of her intelligence, mixed with a healthy dose of over-possessiveness. And though Rees tried to afford Celia privacy, he did know her affection for him was more sibling-like, and tolerant. Rees knew his relationship with Celia went much deeper than anything Brody had ever shown. They were connected right down to each other's souls. Yet he couldn't shake his annoyance, and the heat that crawled up his neck and face.

There.

Along the corner of his vision a fast slinking reptiliiass, no, a wiizelle? Long and slender with four tiny feet. Black as night with a silver sheen mixed in its fur, with bright yellow eyes, moving in and out of the golden-gray shadows. Rees didn't know if the creature was a threat, but Tiimas had made it sound as though all the living things that inhabited the waters below were dangerous.

His heart raced and held tight to Celia's hand despite the slickness of the water making her skin slippery. They swam deeper and faster, hurrying to the bottom of the pond where the butipods were buried. Rees could almost see their destination when a faint muted scream reached his ears from ahead. A cloud of red reached towards them, which spread out and around, blood.

Rees yanked Celia upwards with him in a hurry to evade whatever was coming for them, when he felt Cerviias hand on his shoulder.

"Calm yourself Rees, they're on our side." She spoke to only him.

"Who's on our side? Whoever killed them? How can you tell? How do you know?" Even his own voice in his thoughts sounded alarmed.

"Trust me Rees."

He reached for Cerviias' emotions, tried to feel what she was feeling, looking for deceit, for betrayal. But he found none. Only a sense of earnest honesty.

Rees attempted to soothe the tension that had flooded his body, when a second slightly louder scream, still muffled from the water, and another cloud of red engulfed them. His eyes flitted back and forth looking for the threat. Brody remained, tense, ready, but calm. He wondered if Cerviias had spoken to him as well, it wasn't like Brody to keep a stoic composure.

Moments later Whiisass' body floated up towards them. His breath expelled and therefore bubble helmet gone, eyes open wide yet filmed over and void of life. His white hair pooled around his pearlescent face floating in the waters like a frosted lantern in the darkness of the golden-gray waters. The other guard's body floated up seconds later. Rees could only watch and stare, unable to pull his eyes away or make his mind form words.

Cerviias looked at Rees. "That wiizelle did you a favor, and it's not a threat to us. Those guards had orders from Tiimas to kill all of you once everyone was down here."

☐Rees froze. Struck by the brazenness of Cerviias' words and Tiimas' intended actions. "How would he have gotten away with such a thing? And I thought he wanted the Origin for himself? Killing me would only revert it back to my father."

"Rees, isn't it obvious? Do I need to remind you how delicate and rare the surrogate process is?" Cerviias paused, waiting for an answer. When none came, she continued. "Tiimas wants to eliminate the Origin. He wants to eliminate the monarchy and take Meraiis for himself, as a dictator. Once you were out of the picture, and with your father currently in cogitation for the upcoming transfer, and therefore with less security, it would have been easy to assassinate Fridiias as well." She paused again, searching his eyes for understanding before saying. "He didn't want to risk a very public and very possible failed transfer."

Everything clicked into place. His shock and confusion evaporated replaced by anger. Tiimas had endangered Celia's life with his selfishness, with his greed, and that realization had his vision turning red with rage.

☐Rees took a deep steadying breath, then scooped Celia into his arms and held on tight, fighting against the water that wanted to separate them. Grateful that no harm had come to her... yet. His alertness renewed, looking for the next threat.

☐"Rees."

☐Her eyes were wide, and he almost forgot that she had just witnessed two dead bodies floating past her, and he realized she was crying. Then he sensed her nausea. She couldn't throw up in her bubble, it would burst.

"I know, I know my Star." He felt her jolt slightly from his use of the endearment, but she quickly relaxed against him again, and he continued. "But please, you mustn't be sick down here. You need your air. You need your bubble to hold. Slow, deep breaths. You can do this."

Her body slowly stopped quivering and he could feel the steady rhythm of her heart between their bodies.

"Rees, I'm tired. I don't know how much longer I can keep kicking my legs like this and the pressure is increasing the further we go."

Cerviias caught his questioning gaze and addressed both of them and Brody as well. "We have friends down here. The Aquafisiian's are not the ruthless monsters that Tiimas would have you believe." She gestured to the group. "Come on, follow me."

Little clues ticked the corner of Rees' mind. First Cerviias had come across as a fearful subordinate, but now she was taking charge, and unphased by the death of the two guards. Plus, she wasn't even concerned about the wiizelle that had killed them. Then there was Carl left behind on the surface, he was awful at keeping secrets, yet it was obvious Rees wasn't privy to something happening with him.

But the Origin inside him had never led him astray. The celestial waves could be hidden on occasion, dimmed sometimes, but they could never lie. Cerviias only had goodness pouring out of her aura. The tension Rees had been feeling floated away with the bodies above them.

He nodded, and followed Cerviias down into the depths of the water below.

Chapter Nineteen

She hated being in the dark. And now she was smothered in it, in more ways than one. She could sense there were unshared conversations happening around her. Everyone but her seemed so unphased by the death of the two guards. Her heart pounded frantically, trying to see through the golden gray waters, readying for the next attack. When none came, and her adrenaline faded, the burn in her body returned. She wasn't sure how much longer she could go on swimming like this.

The memory of Rees's voice in her head ran on repeat, soothing her nerves. He had called her, 'his star'. The butterflies flittering in her stomach flew into overdrive. Perhaps he did care for her as much as she cared for him. It was always so hard to know for sure with Rees, he spoke so little, but what he did say was always powerful and meaningful.

It was also difficult to accept her feelings for someone she had known for such a short while. But this tether between them was undeniable, no matter her insecurities, and the numerous ways he had protected her and put her first without question made her feel safe and secure.

Yet at the Capitol he hadn't even wanted to hold her hand at first. No, she shouldn't question that, he explained the difference in the cultures when it came to physical touch, so why was she doubting his affection for her?

Maybe it was the clear and significant history with Dairea. The warm way they had greeted each other, afterall she was his assigned betrothed.

But he was so young when he left.

She knew whatever they had couldn't be anymore than nostalgia. And it was obvious she was with Tiimas now.

But the invasive thoughts kept coming.

That something was shared between Rees and Dairea, as she recalled the way Rees looked away when Dairea kissed Tiimas.

What could that have meant?

Was he jealous?

No.

It was her; Celia was the one that was jealous.

The idea of Rees having a history that did not include her, no matter how irrational, hurt her heart. That, combined with the mixed and unclear signals he always threw her direction had, in part, led to the way she let her fury unleash on him before.

She had hated herself in that moment.

The way her irrationality presented outwardly in such a harmful way towards Rees.

But she had to forgive herself.

Why was she spiraling like this?

It was a lot for anyone to deal with. Seeing and learning so much in such a short amount of time combined with brand new and intense feelings she had never experienced before.

But, it still didn't make sense.

Celia felt like she was losing herself.

Maybe it was the attack. Maybe it triggered something vulnerable in her. She tried to calm herself. To think rationally. This train of thought reminded her of the emotional crash she had when she ran away from the Sanctuary and her responsibilities to Elijah's house. She wasn't herself then either.

The blue rabbit.

There was a commonality between the two, the way she was feeling and the death of the rabbit. She was sure of it.

But just as the thought had entered her mind, it left just as quickly, as if waking from a dream.

Suddenly her mind cleared and the image that filled her vision was when she apologized to Rees at the edge of the pond, and he held her, and sang to her. She thought for sure her heart would explode. All thoughts of jealousy or doubt that hid in the shadows of her mind, were chased away by the light of Rees's touch. The sound of him, and the comfort he provided. She knew without a doubt, in that moment, that she would never leave his side.

Now, here they were. In the dark, swimming into unknown depths together. The cool water slick against her skin, and the shadows wavering in the dark gray and golden light unnerved her.

Something slithered in the corner of her eyesight.

She swam closer to Rees.

"Rees, hold my hand?"

His warm hand enveloped hers.

"Of course, my Star, stay close."

She looked to the right and could faintly see the warmth in Brody's cheeks as his eyes narrowed and his jawline twitched. She cringed a little on the inside. Celia didn't enjoy the effect she had on Brody, but the way he felt about her wasn't her fault. She was always very clear about her feelings towards him. He was her best friend, and she did love him, just not in that way.

When she thought she couldn't kick her legs anymore, they finally reached the bottom of the pond, more lake-like in size and depth, she casually wondered why they called it a pond.

"What now?" Rees telespoke to the group. "We have no tools to dig the butipods up, the guards had all the supplies."

Cerviias replied. "The Aquafisiian will join us soon, they will have all the butipods we need. We wait."

Celia's eyes widened in surprise. "I'm sorry, what or who are the Aquafisiian? I thought we were just harvesting butipods, and now we're meeting someone down here?" Celia ground her teeth and flung her arms out. "And there was hardly surprise from any of you," she pointed to each of them, "that two guards just got murdered!" Her frustrations with being kept in the dark were bubbling to the surface again. "Someone needs to tell me what in the fuck is going on here!" She took a deep slow breath inside her bubble helmet and said calmly. "No more side conversations, please."

Rees gripped her shoulders and looked deeply into her eyes. "You're right, my Star, I'm sorry developments have occurred without your inclusion. I will explain when I can, and I will try harder for transparency going forward. However, I am blind as well when it comes to meeting with the Aquafisiian, it seems there have been silent plans being made on the sidelines." Rees looked pointedly at Cerviias.

Brody took this opportunity, as he always did, to make himself more important to the conversation and by extent, to Celia. He swam close, putting space between her and Rees, then wrapped an arm around her shoulder. "Don't worry, C, I'll keep you safe."

Celia rolled her eyes and Brody chuckled as she shrugged him off. "My hero."

The look of hurt on Rees's face made her stomach roll. Apparently sarcasm didn't always translate well between them. She understood then, in that moment, that perhaps she too had misinterpreted the earlier exchanges between Rees and Dairea. She never wanted Rees to feel the way she felt when she watched Diarea fit so perfectly between Rees's arms when they had greeted each other. She reached for Rees's hand and as their fingers curled into each other, she pulled her body through the water and toward him. The spirals of her hair floated out and around them, encapsulating the two of them in their own little space.

She focused on making sure Rees was the only one she was telespeaking to. "Rees, we have so much to learn about each other's world's still. But please, if you know one thing for sure, know that I care for you, and only you, deeply."

He stopped short of resting his forehead against hers, so as to not burst their helmet bubbles, and his closeness sent her beating heart into a somersault.

Something slithered again just out of direct sight, and they pulled apart quickly. Eyes alert and pulse throbbing, Celia squinted into the darkness of the water.

There.

Behind a bundle of black seaweed, a golden webbed foot emerged. The figure moved forward, walking along the pond floor, not floating, as though gravity was not displaced in water for them the same as it was for others, or perhaps they were much heavier than a human.

Their skin was dark golden and had a mild shine, like liquid gold. They were a bi-ped creature with two legs, and two arms with webbed feet and hands. Their eyes were larger than a humans, dark gray, almost black, and when they blinked their lids closed vertically, much like a lizard. They had large gills on the side of their neck. Short nubs that ended in tiny glowing orbs covered the top of their head like hair. They wore a loose fitting sheer black tunic. It flowed as though it were made of a very fine layer of the black seaweed that filled the pond.

They came to a stop in front of Cerviias and smiled, a mouth full of pointed shiny black teeth, like tiny knives made of obsidian. They spoke out loud to Cerviias in a language Celia had never heard before. Muffled by the water, but unnerving all the same. It sounded like a mix between a screech and a song, what she imagined a siren might sound like from the fantasy books she had read back home. It made her skin crawl and sent a shiver up her spine. This creature was powerful, Celia felt it in her bones.

Brody and Rees waded water on either side of Celia, watching the exchange between this creature and Cerviias. It was clear that Cerviias spoke telepathically, while the creature spoke their language out loud. Celia's body began to quake, when finally, Cerviias swam, and the creature walked over towards them.

"This is our Aquafisiian contact, Chaniia." Cerviias gestured to the creature. "Your breathing helmets will not last much longer, she is going to bestow to you all the gift of aquarespire. Then Chaniia will lead us to Aquatiia."

Panic started to bubble in Celia's chest. *What the hell is aquarespire and what if I don't want it?*

Rees must have been listening to her thoughts again. As soon as she had let her guard down, she could feel their mental connection again, as strong as ever, and she wondered why she had ever blocked him out.

Rees grasped her hands tightly in his. And when he spoke, she could sense he was addressing Brody as well. "I've heard of this process. From what I understand, it will give us gills while we are underwater. The transition will burn, but we will return to normal when we are once again on land."

What the fuck? Give me gills? Celia could feel the wildness within her as she stared into his eyes. "Rees, I don't understand. Why do we have to do all this? Why can't we just dig up a couple butipods, go back to the surface, and then go home?"

He stared at her quizzically. "I thought it was clear when the guards died."

"Rees, nothing about this is clear. Some creature killed them. Yeah it's sad, but it doesn't explain why we have to go to wherever this place is."

She watched his face soften to one of understanding, as though he was realizing once again, that he had failed to translate a key piece on what was happening around them.

"My Star, Tiimas wants me, and the Origin, terminated. It's not safe to return to the surface. At least, not right away."

It was as if a hot poker tore through her back. The edges of her vision blurred and she began to hyperventilate.

"No. No, no, no. What about Carl and Lucy, we can't just leave them up there!" She gripped his arms tightly, struggling for something solid and sure to hold on to. "This is too much, we have to turn back , we have to-"

She was losing air. Celia could see the bubble in front of her eyes move closer and closer to her face.

It was shrinking.

She wanted to run, she wanted to scream. They were so far down, she'd never make it back to the surface in time. Celia was going to suffocate and die. She'd never rid Earth of the evil souls. Her whole family, everything she had ever known would die with her.

She failed.

The Aquafisiian walked towards her. Celia took one last gulp of air and held her breath as the last of the bubble disappeared. Chaniia grabbed one of Celia's hands and placed the tips of her webbed fingers against Celia's human ones. A string of black glowing balls began to move underneath Chaniia's dark golden skin. Dozens of them pulsed from her neck and down her shoulder, and grew in size and quantity as they flew down Chaniia's arm like tiny pulsating lights.

When they reached the tip of Chaniia's webbed hands, Celia felt something small and hot against her skin, like tiny needles were piercing through the tips of her fingers. She reflexively tried to pull away, but Chaniia held on tight. Suddenly the black glowing balls were underneath Celia's skin. They burned as they traveled up her arm to her neck and settled there. Then the burning intensified like hot magma as she felt her skin stretching and tearing around her neck.

Celia let out her last lungful of air as she screamed into the dark waters.

Once that air left her lungs, instinctually she inhaled and she was shocked to find that she could breathe. Chaniia let go, and Celia reached up to feel her throat. There, on both sides, sat rows of gills embedded into Celia's neck. She laughed with relief, and the wonder of it.

Chaniia nodded and smiled with those sharp pointed teeth as she walked over to Brody who appeared more shocked than she had ever seen him before. He cautiously allowed Chaniia to place her webbed hands against his and repeated the process for him, and then Rees.

The water around her felt lighter, like air, and Celia found herself sinking to the pond floor, no longer needing to swim.

This is fucking cool!

She smiled to herself and twirled against the water, allowing herself the momentary relief of forgetting all their troubles, and taking in another of the astounding wonders of Meraiis.

Chapter Twenty

The dark golden waters that surrounded her, clouding her vision, had been cleared by the gift of aquarespire. Celia glanced behind her at Rees, Brody, and Cerviias with her bright white hair sticking straight up in the water like a pale blue flame atop her head. Their eyes had all transformed to that of the Aquafisiian, large, dark gray nearly black, and blinking vertically. A chill ran up her spine at the sight of them. They were still clearly themselves, but foreign in an eerie way. The realization had her hand flying to her teeth, scared to find tiny obsidian knives there, but gratefully her teeth were still hers, human.

She tried not to focus on the unnatural feeling it gave her to see them all transformed, ignoring the shiver that ran down her back.

She focused instead on the natural wonders all around her as they walked along a smooth pebbled path on the pond floor, following Chaniia. With clear sight Celia could better appreciate the variations of plantae. All she had seen before of Aquatiia were the thickets of black seaweed. Now, so many hidden wonders made themselves known.

Tube-like translucent plants grew against the rocks that dotted the area, floating in the water as though they were waving at them. Worm-like creatures floated above their heads like a school of fish. Stretching and shrinking as they swam, partly transparent like the plants, but also mildly color changing, as though they had built in camouflage.

The slinking shadows that had crossed her vision moments before her transformation, the things responsible for the death of the guards, were now out in the open. Celia had thought there were multiple of these creatures hunting them, she could see now it was only one very fast moving creature. It looked like an Earth weasel, but built for the water like a skinny beaver with a fluffy tail. Celia's heart ticked up a notch and her breathing came in rapidly at the sight of it. Would it attack her too?

Chaniia spoke calmly to her mind. "Calm yourself human, it's only my wiizelle, its name is Flouiita and it only kills on my command."

Celia didn't find that nearly as reassuring as she was sure it was supposed to be.

Chaniia called to it then with a high pitched screech of a whistle, and the thing came hurtling to her side like a slick bullet that wrapped its long body twice around her shoulders and settled there. It was somewhat cute in an alarming sort of way with its four tiny feet and silver sheen in its black fur, if only its bright yellow eyes didn't drink her in like an exotic snack for the taking.

Celia hung back a few steps to align herself by Rees's side. She reached for his hand and he happily allowed it, clasping his fingers against hers, squeezing her hand tight. Celia couldn't ignore the scoff she heard from Brody behind them.

She turned to glare at him. "Oh mind your own business, Brody." And she gasped at the sound that came out of her, squeezing Rees tighter and clamping her other hand across her mouth. It was high pitched with a slight screech, and it echoed, no longer muffled, as though they were not surrounded by water, but in a very large empty cave.

It unsettled Celia, that sound. To have her own words come from her mouth, yet it wasn't the familiarity of her own voice. Brody laughed at her and shook his head as they continued to walk. Celia looked away grinding her teeth, but relaxed when Rees comforted her by letting go of her hand and wrapping an arm around her waist, pulling her close. "No matter my Star, remember, you will be yourself again soon enough." Celia took comfort in his reassurance, finding warmth in the weight of his body next to hers.

They followed Chaniia along the path for a while longer until the rock formations grew in size and shape. No longer little piles of rock with plants growing on them, but it seemed as though they were walking in between underwater mountains, and those outcroppings of sea stacks had been shaped and smoothed into something familiar to Celia that she couldn't quite place. The stacks began to take on a clearer shape, as though they had been molded into tall reaching homes. Celia thought to her mental catalog of books from home, only one word came to mind. Skyscrapers. The rock formations were exactly like the pictures she had seen of giant glass buildings that shone against the sunlight. She drank in the wonder of it all. Imposing and majestic, making her feel small under the shadow of the marvelous city.

Within these underwater towers, some freestanding and some snug against the larger mountains, there came a glow, like bioluminescent electricity. She was reminded of the eels of Earth she had learned of. Their glowing eyes peered out of glass-less windows all the way to the tops, but all unmoving.

She asked Chaniia in her mind. "Are those lights living creatures?"

Chaniia startled, as though Celia's question was an intrusion in her mind. Nevertheless, she grimaced but answered her question. "No. Only the surface dwellers enslave living things. Those 'things' that you call lights are Amphiiura, a type of plantae, they are grown along all the homes of Aquatiia. They only appear to have a face."

Celia nodded in amazement, and made a mental note that the Aquafisiian might not appreciate unsolicited teletalk. She leaned her head against Rees's shoulder in an effort to chase away the chill of Chaniia's sharp tongue.

Chaniia telespoke to them all. "We are close. We'll meet and arrange a path forward."

"Thank you for your partnership." Cerviias responded. "Your honorable actions will not soon be forgotten."

Chaniia came to a sudden halt, and turned to face Cerviias. "Our kind are not guided by accolades such as honor and remembrance, we are simply attempting to preserve the integrity of the planet by aligning with the group we believe will cause the least amount of harm. Our only goal is the protection of our Meraiis, as yours should be. Alas, you fight amongst yourselves for petty reasons. Risking the health of us all." She paused, glaring at them. "If it were up to me, I'd have you all exterminated." She waved her arms in defeat. "But as father says, that only makes us as bad as them." She shook her head and continued leading the way. "Whatever that means."

They continued to follow her. It was suddenly very clear to Celia where all of Chaniia's angst was coming from. If she were honest with herself, she could understand her way of thinking. Afterall, Celia's home was nothing more than a sample size of Earth, trapped inside a dome, sitting on Meriias, and that small slice was precious to her kind.

It was all they had left.

From what she had learned in her history lessons, even if the meteor hadn't destroyed the rest of Earth, it was dying anyway, even after the fresh start her birth had given the planet. Humans had fucked it all up again with their poisonous hate. Celia was surprised by the anger deep within her bubbling to the surface. These overwhelming and unwanted sensations were sneaking up on her more often.

It worried her.

She pushed the feeling back down, burying it within her. Now was not the time to think about herself, she had a home to save.

As they got closer to what seemed like the center of the city, more Aquafisiian's showed themselves. Staring at their small group as they passed with curious faces. They traveled through what must be a kind of market place.

The Aquafisiian traded more of the clothes like what Chaniia wore, made of the sheer black seaweed but in various styles and shades. A variety of foods that were alien to Celia also filled the space, along with other items that she could not place. As they left the market behind, they headed to what appeared to be the center of the city, and as they made progress the towers grew in size, until they came to the tallest one of all and stopped in front of it.

Chaniia turned to face them. "Your arrogance as a species," she paused, looking at Celia pointedly before continuing, "both of your species, is unmatched. Please attempt a molecule of respect. My father's heart may be bigger than mine, but he is no servant to your whims."

Cerviias bowed her head in reverence, hands clasped behind her back, acknowledging the seriousness of her words.

Chaniia pressed her webbed hand against a spot on the solid wall, and a door shaped slab of it sank down into the ground below, a billow of sand swirling in the water as they crossed the threshold. Once through, Chaniia turned and placed her palm again against the wall and the slab rose back into place. The hallways were wide, tall, elongated ovals, with multiple rooms and corridors leading off the main hall as they made their way, all lit by the Amphiiura. The building didn't appear to have any seams, as though the entirety of the tower was a mountain, carved and shaped to fit the needs of the Aquafisiian.

After a couple of minutes they stopped in front of one of the many doors. Chaniia opened it the same way as the main entrance, and Celia hesitantly followed her in. Inside the spacious room, there was a long oval table carved from more of the mountain, and a dozen simple stone chairs.

At the head of the table sat an imposing figure, one whom Celia could only assume was Chaniia's father. He stood, his demeanor much more welcoming than Chaniia's, a smile on his face showing his rows of obsidian teeth. The glowing nubs on his head were longer than his daughters, appearing almost like hair, and unlike his daughters lustrous golden skin, his was paler, tarnished somehow as if showing his age.

"Welcome my surface friends." He spread his arms wide. "Please, have a seat. We have much to discuss, and very little time to do so."

"Thank you Ezekiia." Cerviias bowed. "For your assistance and hospitality during this trying time."

Ezekiia smiled and nodded, then gestured for them all to take a seat. Celia, Brody, and Rees all exchanged hesitant looks, but cautiously sat down.

Cerviias addressed the room. "Forgive me, but before we begin, the rest of my party-" she gestured to them, "have been woefully in the dark. I must bring them to light of the situation we face."

Ezekiia gave her a short nod and turned his body to the side, as if to give them a moment of semi-privacy. Chaniia ran her gray tongue over her obsidian teeth, and rolled her eyes, as though she had much better things to be doing than having a meet and greet with topsiders.

Cerviias clasped her hands in front of her on the table and looked Celia in the eyes, then to Rees, and Brody.

"Your father–"

Celia saw Rees clench his jaw. She reached out for his hand and they laced their fingers again.

"Has not become as evil as he may seem." Cerviia's gills flared on the side of her neck as she took a deep breath. "He did sentence you to death, but he had planned to break you out and set you free before the sentence could be carried out."

Rees squeezed her hand tighter and she wanted to wrap him in a hug, but held herself still. Instead she brushed her thumb along the side of his hand, in what she hoped was a comforting gesture.

Cerviias continued. "All those years ago, when you were banished and your mother defended you... it was not your father who ordered her execution. The Duiistian clan, Ti-imas's line, demanded it. They planned to go after you as well, but your father thwarted them, and he knew then that the only way to save you, Redreesishual, was to retain his power and keep the Duiistian clan under his thumb. And so, you were banished to satisfy them, and save your life."

Celia spared a glance at Rees, and if she had to guess, she'd say he had tears in his eyes. It was hard to tell, being underwater. But the emotion on his face was clear. She squeezed his hand tighter and rubbed his arm for warmth before she looked back to Cerviias.

"The moment you stepped foot in the Capitol, your father knew you were in danger. He's been planning your rescue since that moment. Those of us who are loyal to him, know the truth. Your father does not care to take back the Origin, he only cares for you."

Rees shook his head, disbelief lacing his features. "But, you worked for Tiimas. You were his servant, you were scared of upsetting him when I spoke to you."

Cerviias nodded. "Yes, I began working for Tiimas many years ago, at the appointment of your father. I was meant to spy on the Duiistian clan and report back. Your father has far reaching allies." She paused and gestured to Ezekiia. "And he has been stretching himself thin, using celestial waves for communication, all to save you. His son. Who he loves very much."

Rees's body began to shake in heavy sobs, and Celia could no longer keep herself from wrapping her arms around his shoulders. His head nuzzled into the curve of her neck, and she held on tight while he let his cries out.

When Rees's last tears finally fell, and his body calmed, Celia returned back to her chair, but still held tightly to his hand.

"I know this is a lot to take in Rees." Cerviias said. "But if you remember one thing, remember that your father fought for you. He was never able to succeed in his plans to make Meraiis a better planet. He doesn't agree with the division within our society. But he does believe that you have that power. That you can be the one who tips the scales back to the side of morality. That you have more goodness in you than anyone he's ever seen. That you are the rightful carrier of the Origin."

Brody leaned forward from his seat and a thick screech came out of him, as though he were clearing his throat.

"Well, I'm glad prince charming over here is having an emotional revelation and all. But there's still the matter of our friends topside, our home on the brink of collapse from evil souls, and how in the hell are we going to get out of this underwater hellhole."

"BRODY!" Celia glared at him. "Read the room for fucks sake!"

He returned her glare. "Oh don't start with me, I know you'd be focused on the same things if you weren't so concerned for lover boy here."

Bubbles gurgled from Chaniia's mouth and her shoulders shook with laughter. "Hey, I might like this human." She said as she continued to chortle.

Ezekiia stood again, facing them all. "Yes. The plan. Your father's allies have been in communication with another member of your team, Carl, I believe he is called. He had instructions on when and where to slip away with your friend Lucy. We have a store of butipods ready for you to take, and we have an escape tunnel that will lead you out of this so-called 'hellhole' popping you out topside to meet with your friends. That's where we'll leave you. The rest of your journey, I'm afraid, is on your shoulders to bear."

He gestured to his daughter and continued. "Chaniia will guide you through the escape tunnel. But I'm afraid the journey is long and you must gather yourself some rest."

Brody stood, crossing his arms across his chest and shaking his head. "Your honor, or whatever in the hell I'm supposed to call you, I'm not tired, and we don't exactly have time to spare. We need to be on our way."

Ezekiia made eye contact with Celia. "I'm afraid the same can't be said for your companion."

Celia felt her cheeks warm. She wished what Ezekiia said wasn't true. But they spent so long swimming, her whole body ached. And if what he said was true about it being a difficult journey, she could use all the rest they'd give her.

Brody's face softened when he looked at her, as though seeing her exhaustion for the first time. Not all of us can have super strength. She thought to herself, and Rees must have heard because he glanced at her as he gave her hand a gentle squeeze.

Brody rolled his eyes. "Fine. But just a short rest, C."

Celia gave him a soft smile and nodded.

"Very well." Ezekiia said. "Chaniia will show you to your sleeping quarters."

They all followed Chaniia out of the meeting room. In the quiet of their walk, her mind turned and body shook, Celia's stomach knotted at the thought of what was next to come.

Chapter Twenty-One

The cold rocks scraped against her forearms as she crawled through the tunnel leading to the surface, leaving a burning sensation in their wake. Aquaspire had not only given her the gift of breathing underwater, but also a heaviness as though she were not swimming, but on solid dry ground. That also made trekking through the water filled lava tube, more of a hike than a swim.

She copied every foot and handhold of Brody in front of her, who copied Cerviias leading the way. Rees followed behind Celia, which brought some comfort, but her nerves still itched under her skin knowing Chaniia and her pet wizelle, Flouiita were behind them all. With the butipods safely tucked inside her pack, Celia was anxious to leave behind the sidelong glances of the Aquafisiian and get home to her family, and the Sanctuary.

After what felt like hours, their steady incline became less strenuous. Slowly, the feeling of floating began to return. The gills on the sides of her neck started to flare, as though each breath of water was a fiery blaze in her throat. Her underwater vision became blurry and out of focus. Each step forward was more difficult than the last, as she pushed her body to move against the pressure of water closing in on them.

When she finally caught tendrils of light at the end of the tunnel, excitement flooded within her, only to be dashed in an instant when a sharp pain pierced her calf. A cry tore through her and a cloud of inky red billowed around her. Celia's heart raced as she searched for the threat through bleary eyes.

For a half second Celia caught a flame of anger in Rees's eyes when she looked behind her, but it was quickly blocked by a fresh wave of crimson water and another bout of pain from her other calf.

It was Chaniia's pet that had attacked her. Its small, slick body was able to navigate around them.

Chaniia remained behind Rees, but her voice filled Celia's mind. "Let this be a warning to you and your people. You are not wanted here. My father may be a man of peace, but I am not."

A flash of golden skin and obsidian teeth appeared behind Rees, giving one last look of warning before she quickly disappeared, Chaniia was gone, no doubt making her way back home. Celia couldn't feel her tears as they fell on her face through the water, but she felt them in her chest.

Rees's alarm mixed with rage, rang clear as a bell in her head. "Celia, my Star, are you okay?"

"No- I don't know. Flouiita attacked me?"

Rees didn't respond, but when she craned her neck to look at him the answer sat clearly on his face. He wrapped an arm around her middle and tugged her upward. Celia used all the strength she could muster and pulled herself up with him. Another wave of pain from her neck and lungs fought for attention as her head broke through the surface of the water.

She had expected to emerge somewhere close to where they had entered the Aquafisiian territory, but it was obvious by the intense blast of cold air, that their group was in a completely different part of Meraiis. Celia clawed her way out of the opening, grasping handfuls of frozen crumbling wetness. Snowflakes stuck to her wet eyelashes. Rees pushed her from behind, and Brody grabbed hold of her arms and pulled her the rest of the way out of the tube.

Her surroundings were still blurred, and each breath of air was sharp in her lungs like thousands of tiny pointed needles as her body adjusted back to human. Brody's voice was muddled, as if they were still underwater and not sitting at the top of a cold mountain. Celia shook her head, trying to clear the fog away.

Rees's voice rang sharp in her mind. "My Star, are you okay? Can you hear me?"

She tried to answer, but the words fell from her mouth, mumbled. An air of panic surrounded her. A feminine voice, to her left danced to her ears as Celia felt her head sway.

Lucy? She thought to herself.

"The wizelle, it's bite is venomous." No, not Lucy, she wouldn't know that. Must be Cerviias then. Her feminine voice echoed to her ears as consciousness threatened to evade Celia.

Someone grabbed her from behind, under the arms, to pull her further away from the hole in the ground. Steam rose from the opening, but the further she was dragged, the colder she became. Her body shivered and her teeth chattered. Every breath a torch in her chest. Her legs, nothing more than hot rubbery extensions of her body filled with millions of tiny pin pricks.

Celia nodded in and out of consciousness.

A vision of tar-like thick water flooding and thunderous as it rushed the forest surrounding the Sanctuary, was the last thing her mind saw as Celia succumbed to the darkness.

Chapter Twenty-Two

Consciousness slowly returned to Celia.

She tried to open her eyes, but found them stuck together. She gingerly touched them and found crustiness across her lids. They were sealed shut with dried goop excreted from her tear ducts. She carefully peeled her eyes open, slowly, and with great effort. She experienced this once before when she had pink eye as a child. Her mother had used a warm wet cloth to gently clean away the goop. Celia's process however, was anything but gentle.

Pinching pain pierced her with each millimeter as if small pins held her eyes closed and the flesh and lashes tore as she forced herself awake. She took tremendous care, as much as she could anyway, riding herself of the confining crust.

With her eyes now tender, but finally open, she tried to make out something familiar; a face, shape, or sound, but only blurred grayness and silence surrounded her. Her limbs were heavy and her mouth dry. She tried to lift her head, but gravity pushed against her, the traitorous thing.

Fuck you gravity.

Celia sunk back to the ground with a groan. As her breathing slowed, she could hear a fire crackling in the distance. Her vision cleared after a few more blinks, and that's when she noticed the high pile of furs on top of her. She reached an arm out to the side and felt cold stone under her fingertips.

She tried to call out for Rees but only coarse air escaped her lips. Fresh hot tears of frustration leaked down the sides of her face and pooled in her ears.

Finally, hope leapt in her chest at the sound of hard footsteps echoing to her ears, followed soon after by panic. Who do the footsteps belong to? Her fear built as the sound grew closer with each step.

Move.

Her arms and legs wouldn't listen to her brain. Sure, she could move them. Feel, touch, make small movements, peel her eyelids open. But she was so weak, and the air was so heavy, neither her arms nor her legs would support her weight. It was like she was under some sort of spell. Every time she tried, she failed to sit or stand. She was infuriatingly stuck in her own body.

She suddenly recalled the story of the Princess and the Goblin. She imagined some green, slimy, wart-filled little troll coming to scoop her brains out and make a stew. The footsteps stopped.

Shit.

"My Star, you're awake!"

Ah, thank you Gods.

Celia chuckled with relief. "You're not a troll!" But her voice did not sound like her voice.

"What?" Rees kneeled down, looking at her with a furrowed brow and smoothed her hair, then shouted over his shoulder. "Celia's awake but something's wrong, she's not making any sense, hurry."

Wait, did I just understand him without telepathy?

Incredulous, she laughed again. "No. I'm fine." Celia's tongue, still thick and dry, kept her from forming clear words. "Well, not fine." Her voice was becoming increasingly incoherent, hoarse, and faint.

Where the hell is the mind reading when you need it.

Their connection clearly weakened as much as her body, she normally would have sensed it was Rees coming towards her. Felt his energy before she saw him. Celia slowed her breathing, and focused.

With all her might, she formed a single, clear, word. "Water."

Rees nodded, panic in his eyes before he disappeared from view.

He didn't seem to notice that she had spoken the word in Meraiin. Celia's thoughts raced as she tried to understand what was happening to her. It had to be a side-effect of the wizelle venom, it must have severed their connection. Why then, was she suddenly able to speak their language? It didn't make sense.

The fear and uncertainty bubbling within her was threatening to overflow, so she distracted herself by looking more at her surroundings. It appeared they were in a cave system. The rounded stone room Celia occupied was bare. No furnishings, definitely not a home. They must still be in the wilds of Meraiis. Light came from the walls themselves. She had never seen such a thing. There were narrow veins of glowing orange criss-crossing across the entire surface like a spider's web.

Her stomach dropped and swayed; what she imagined it might feel like to be on a boat. It felt eerily similar to the descriptions of the yellow-bellied scoundrels she read about in her pirate books. Just when Celia thought she might be sick, Rees returned with a canteen of water. He carefully held her head up and placed it against her lips. She took slow small sips until her mouth felt familiar again.

"Thank you." She said.

Rees's eyes bugged out, surprise etched in every line of his features. "Can you understand me?"

She managed a small nod of her head and a smile. Rees was quiet for several seconds before saying. "But I can no longer reach your mind. Can you connect with mine?"

She shook her head slowly and a single tear, leftover from her torn lids, slid down her cheek.

He caressed her cheek and that's when his eyes went wide again. "Oh, my Star, your eyes are bleeding."

Okay, not tears, blood.

He reached behind himself and came back with a rag in hand. He dampened it with water from the canteen and gingerly began dabbing at her eyes. "Does it hurt my Star?" He asked.

She ground her teeth in response and managed an acknowledging moan of assent.

After he finished cleansing her eyes as best he could, he reached within his billowing black robes and pulled out a small container of green goo, and carefully applied it to her eyes. Immediate relief soothed her skin and she realized then how tense her body had become from the pain.

As she relaxed, Rees asked. "Better?"

She nodded. "Yes. I'm nauseous though, and hot. Can you help get these furs off of me?"

"Of course my Star." He replied. "I need to grab your clothing though."

"I'm naked!?" Celia could feel it then. The dry hides of the fur rubbing roughly against her skin, and unpleasant shivers ran up her spine.

"Yes. You were soaked after the tunnel, and we are at a high altitude in the middle of a winter storm, we had to get you warm." Rees said nonchalantly. She was fastly reminded how straight forward and emotionless he could be. A trickle of anger spread through her, but she bit it back. She knew he was only trying to take care of her.

Rees stepped out of her sight and returned with a bundle of her clothing. He averted his eyes as much as possible while he removed each layer of fur. Celia was appreciative of the effort on his part. When only one fur remained, he went to stand but she grabbed hold of his wrist. His eyes shot to her hand wrapped around him.

Celia spoke softly. "I'm sorry." She released him. "But I don't think I can dress myself, I can't even stand."

His eyes bore into hers and she could see the longing behind them. She expected him to start helping her, but ever the gentleman he said. "I'll go grab Lucy to assist you, will that be alright my Star?"

She was a little disappointed to be denied such an intimate touch as Rees dressing her. But knew it must be too soon for him, and she smiled. "Yes, thank you, Rees."

He gave her a curt nod and walked away.

Her heart was cold without their constant connection wrapping her up like a warm hug.

She missed him already.

Lucy's soft footsteps entered the chamber. Moments later her short purple hair and bright green eyes were hovering over Celia, hands on her hips.

"So, I hear you're dying." Lucy said sarcastically with a glint of humor in her voice. "If you ask me, I think you just enjoy people fawning over you."

Celia chuckled, causing her dry throat to send her into a fit of coughing.

Lucy laughed. "Okay woman! You don't have to be so dramatic about it, I'll help ya alright." Lucy winked before grabbing the canteen and holding it to Celia's lips. "Better?"

Celia nodded and croaked out her thanks. Lucy grabbed hold of Celia's arms and helped her to a sitting position, then helped her into her shirt. Lucy then pulled Celia's pants on as high as she could before helping her to a stand to tug them up all the way. Celia felt completely useless, a stranger in her own skin. Every part of her body hurt, but was numb and heavy at the same time, such an odd and nonsensical feeling.

Celia mumbled her thanks, then asked. "How long was I out?"

"A couple of days." Lucy replied. "We're almost out of the mountains. Shouldn't be much longer now."

"I'm glad you're here." Celia was genuinely appreciative of Lucy. She had a comfortable energy about her, straight-forward yet kind, trustworthy. "I'm assuming Carl made it too?"

Lucy nodded. "Yep. Turns out your boyfriend's pops is pretty resourceful. He's been feeding Carl and I info for days through the celestial waves."

"Pops?" Celia asked.

"Yeah." Lucy replied. "You never heard the term before? Rees's dad."

"Ah-" Celia's mind caught up with the rest of what Lucy was saying. "Wait. A couple of days? Have you all been carrying me?"

Lucy laughed. "Ah, girl! You're gonna get a kick out of this... we're inside a Petraiim. I call this one Bob, but I don't think it really appreciates-"

Celia cut her off. "A what?"

Lucy chuckled again. "A Petraiim. It's wild Celia. We are inside a living, breathing- well not breathing, I don't think it even has lungs."

"Luce!"

"Right, sorry, I ramble. We're inside a rock giant. He's like the size of two enormous trees stacked, I don't know, twenty-four feet tall maybe?" Lucy's warm hands clasped Celia's, looking her in the eyes. "Rees's dad arranged it all. Bob was there to pick Carl and I up, and we made it to the tunnel just as you all emerged." She grinned. "We're making killer time! Ol' Bob's got a long stride."

Celia's head swam. We're inside a rock giant? That would explain the swaying sensation in her gut, she was motion sick.

Lucy gently tugged on Celia's elbow. "Come on. Let's get you to the heart, it keeps us all warm. And everyone's dying to see you. Especially Brody. Dudes like a pit bull, won't shut up about you."

Celia grinned. She normally would be annoyed by Brody's overprotectiveness, but after everything they'd been through, knowing he was there, worrying about her every move was almost a comfort.

With Lucy carrying her more than she was walking, they made their way down a rock hallway with its glowing orange veins lighting the way, their footsteps echoing around them. They emerged into a large rounded room with a giant orange ball in the center that made a crackling noise like fire. This room was significantly warmer. It appeared to be made of something like crystal quartz with a smooth translucent surface, and the orange center flowed and twirled like liquid hot magma. The hot orange veins of lava all originated from this; the rock giant's heart.

Celia's eyes widened in astonishment. "It's amazing." She glanced around the room to see her friends all engrossed in conversation that stopped when they saw her. Brody was the first to rush towards her, wrapping her up into a tight hug.

"Cee. Thank Gods you're okay. How are you feeling?" Brody asked.

Celia grimaced in his embrace and he pulled away. She answered. "Like I lost about a dozen fist fights. Everything is sore, and heavy. But my motor skills are slowly coming back."

Brody's whole body tensed. "I swear, If I ever meet that damned Chaniia and her fucking pet again, I'm going to-"

Celia groaned in annoyance. "Brody. That's enough. I don't need you to defend my honor, or whatever, just chill the fuck out."

Brody backed away like she had slapped him. "Whatever Cee, so sorry I give a shit." He shook his head and walked away.

Rees, who had silently been watching the entire exchange with his arms crossed and eyes narrowed, glanced at Celia. He slowly walked towards her and whispered in her ear. "Are you okay my Star?"

"I'm fine." She replied stiffly in Meraiin.

Every jaw in the room, with the exception of Rees, dropped.

Someone was about to say something when a deep rumbling sound vibrated the floor. The sound, low and reverberating like gravel grinding against each other, filled their ears.

When the sound stopped Rees said. "That was Briibobert, he says we're approaching the Earthlings border.

"Good Ol' Bob." Lucy said with a smile. "Coming in clutch."

Chapter Twenty-Three

As Lucy's voice trailed away a new sound filled Celia's ears. It was similar to that of rushing water, but louder and thicker, thunderous... crunchier. Like a running rock giant... or maybe a dozen.

Something was coming.

Celia tried to ask the others if they heard it, but her voice was caught in her throat like a trap. She tried again to speak, but failed.

Bob kept moving.

Horror unspooled within Celia the more she tried and failed to talk.

Then something else, or rather a lack of something else, registered in Celia's mind.

Rees just told Cerviias that they were minutes away from Earth's territory.

The close approach to the Sanctuary border should have filled Celia with excitement, anticipation, relief... anything.

But the only thing residing inside herself was an all consuming numbness. She had felt it growing from the moment she had awakened, and now, it was a waterfall rushing her recklessly and without control over the side of a cliff. The desensitized feeling filled her like a crazed shadow covering her from head to toe, and at the center sat a desperate need to accomplish an important task, a task that she was somehow not privy to. Like a job she couldn't remember committing to, nevertheless, she was determined to complete this unrecognizable mission.

Somewhere deep down she knew something was wrong. She could sense the problem like a loose thread waiting to be unraveled, but it was just out of reach in the corner of her mind. She couldn't grab the mental thread no matter how hard she tried. Her body no longer belonged to her, and with each step closer to home she could feel her consciousness slipping away as well.

She was no longer in control of her body, and she was slowly losing control of her mind as well.

Celia was possessed.

Yet the tiniest sliver of hope shined, like the sun reflecting off the surface of a single grain of sand on a vast beach. That hope was fear. Somewhere tucked into a deep pocket, Celia still felt fear. She was terrified that she was close to losing herself entirely, and that speck of emotion was enough to keep her from becoming irrevocably lost.

She did not have the strength to fight for control of her autonomy, but she did have the strength to hold onto her fear.

Celia could not explain how, or when, but at some point Bob had been sucked into the numb shadow with her. It was as though they were of one mind, yet that mind was not in their control. They were puppets with a hidden master.

The other rock giants knew it.

Whoever was in control of her mind and Bob's spoke not only Meraiin but the Petraiim language as well. The rock giant battle cries spoke of defending not only their home territory, but the planet. Their voices were like liquid gravel, rough, loud, and fluid. Celia agreed with them, she needed to be stopped no matter the cost, and if she couldn't stop herself maybe one of the rock giants would be able to. A flood of emotions bubbled beneath the surface of the numb controlling shadow when the thoughts of not being able to say goodbye struck her. Rees. Her parents. Her friends.

Celia watched through Bob's eyes as the other Petraiim rushed towards Briibobert with a swiftness surprising for solid masses of living rock. Their speed generated the sound of an enormous rock slide crashing through the valley and approaching them faster than Celia would have thought possible.

The sight of them filled Celia with overwhelming terror so strong she felt sick. Herself, and her friends were inside Bob, and all of them were about to be smashed to smithereens. But Briibobert was the biggest Petraiim, and whoever was currently in control of Bob was strategic. She could visualize her puppet masters thoughts, precise, and ruthless.

She watched through Bob's eyes as he tore a limb off one of the smaller Petraiim, orange lava spitting from the torn appendage as Bob used it as a weapon. Swinging the rock arm left and right, bashing it into the other Petraiim as they tried to stop Bob from crossing the border. Bob caught sight of one of the Petraiim out of the corner of his eye about to attack, and he shifted so fast his vision swam and the next thing Celia saw was Bob ripping the head from a giant and gushes of magma flowing down its headless body.

Bob kicked the next attacker, his foot going straight through the Petraiims center. Its rock crystal magma filled ball, its heart, fell to the ground and rolled. Bright orange scattered the area like nauseating blooms of unnatural flora. The puddles of rock giant blood cooled and hardened like rust right before their eyes.

It didn't take long for Bob to defeat them all. Celia could feel a new emotion separate from her own, yet it didn't belong to their master, it belonged to Bob. It was agony. A heartbreak so strong it could crumble empires.

He had just unwillingly murdered members of his own family.

The pain was so deep Celia could feel Bob's hatred of self, and his desire to end his own life, but also his inability to do so.

Celia's sight switched to that of her own. Her friends were standing before her. They hadn't seen what Celia saw. They were panicked and talking amongst themselves trying to understand why they were being jostled and why Bob had gone silent. Celia tried to speak to them, to cry, to scream, to warn them, but nothing came out.

Lucy gently patted Celia's arm, the feeling barely registering through the numb shadow. Rees stared at her like a puzzle he was trying to solve.

That gave Celia hope.

Surely he must know. But he turned his gaze from her to talk to Cerviias in their native tongue. Celia realized he must be translating to the humans in their minds, because they all seemed to be following the conversation.

"It seems we were just in battle." Rees said. "I can no longer hear Bob, but I could hear our attackers." He paused, taking a deep worried breath. "Their battle cries spoke of ridding Meraiin of evil, and doing what must be done."

Celia watched his eyes, she knew he was thinking through the meanings of the Petraiim, but her hope faltered when Rees spoke again.

"I presume the other Petraiim were of the same mindset of Chaniia." He said. "I suspect they were trying to stop us from saving the humans. They must think the same, that Meraiis would be better off if the humans died out."

Celia wanted to shout, 'No! You've got it all wrong! It's me they were trying to kill, it's me that's harboring evil. Kill me!' but nothing came out. She unwillingly nodded in agreement with Rees.

Rees spoke again to Cerviias, "We're moments away from the border, we must prepare to disembark from our friend, Bob."

The panic within Celia reached an all time high. They mustn't let Celia go home. Her friends had to realize something was wrong, they had to stop Celia. If the puppet master was strong enough to make Bob kill his own family, what would the master make Celia do to her people? Everyone and everything she loved was at risk. Couldn't Rees sense it? Why didn't he realize something was wrong?

"We're here. We made it." Rees said with a smile on his face.

Celia's stomach dropped.

She was the fox and the man she loved was about to let her into the hen house.

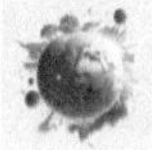

From the moment Celia had opened her eyes after the wiizelle attack Rees knew... of course he knew.

How could he not notice the sudden emptiness, the lack of her essence intermingled with his soul. He ached for her. But speaking to her, and looking into her clear gray eyes, Celia was still there, at least a part of her was, it wasn't too late, not yet. Celia had his whole heart, and he wasn't going to let whatever evil soul possessed her steal her away.

Rees had hope that he could still save her, but he needed help.

How could he alert the others without also alerting the possessor? The evil souls had been on this planet for twenty years, floating from unexpecting brain to unexpecting brain, they almost always knew every language on this planet.

Rees had to keep up the act of his ignorance. If he let his guard down and the evilness inhabiting his beloved Star noticed, it could attack them all, or even worse, force Celia to end her own life. He had to tread carefully. He couldn't risk anything happening to Celia, he'd never survive losing her.

His only chance was reaching the Earth border in time. They'd plant the butipods, which grew instantaneously taking only minutes to reach full height. They would excrete their Cinis ash and excise the evil soul from Celia's body.

But what if that's exactly what the possessor wanted? To get within Earth's border inside the body of their princess, because that's essentially who Celia is to them, right? Perhaps they didn't use that term, but that's what she was, their princess; being groomed to take over governing the Sanctuary for her parents someday.

Everything turned over again and again in his mind, then..

Bob went silent too.

No.

It was quiet for a moment, then the crunch of liquid gravel as Bob ran. Rees could hear the other Petraiim in his mind, shouting their war cries and heartbreak of needing to stop Bob. The other Petraiim, Bob's family, knew the moment he went silent, and unlike Rees, they reacted swiftly and without restraint, but it would cost them their lives. Briibobert was stronger, faster, and crueler under the control of the evil soul.

Rees looked around the heart chamber, the panic in everyone's eyes, their screams as they were thrown side to side with each impact. The battle lasted only minutes, but it left them all shaken. Bloody noses, raw scratches, blooming bruises.

There was no longer a question in Rees's mind. He must stop this evil soul, no matter the cost. Celia would never forgive him if her entire species, her friends, her family were eliminated all because he couldn't let her go.

The realization left him cold, and numb.

His jaw tightened and acid built in his throat. His legs lost their strength as if he would collapse against a soft breeze.

To gain entrance to the rock giant, Bob had quite literally swallowed them. So, they couldn't get out the same way they got in. Bob would have had to reach his hand down his throat to pull them out. But Rees doubted whoever was in control of the giant was willing to let them leave.

How then?

The idea hit his stomach hard, nausea rose within him.

Sacrifice one for the many.

But that was never his philosophy. Save them all no matter the cost was how he had always operated in his life. But now, his soulmate was at risk. Could he really allow her, and the entire Earthling community go extinct?

"Rees!" Lucy shouted at him. She pulled herself up from the stone floor where she had been thrown during the battle, like being thrown inside a ship during a raging ocean storm.

"What in the fuck is going on? We're here, right? Why aren't we getting off this ride from hell?"

Rees didn't know how to answer without giving anything away. He'd have to speak. The evil in control of Bob could hear their thoughts, but maybe it wouldn't be able to hear their voices while they were deep inside the rock giant. He had been practicing the Earth language. Their words tumbled around his tongue, lacking the graceful flow of his native language. These words were foreign, harsh, and unnatural in his mouth.

"Yes, we're here, but we've been in a battle. There's no time to explain." He glanced around the chamber room in a panic. "Do you all trust me?"

They stared at him, a flash of hesitation in their eyes before nodding quickly.

He acknowledged them with a quick tilt of his head.

"CLIMB!" He shouted.

They stood frozen, confused.

He took a deep breath and said as quickly as he could. "I'm going to blow up Bob's heart." He eyed the glowing magma filled ball in the center of the chamber, the rock giant's heart. "You all need to climb the walls now." He said with a fierce edge to his voice, expression dire.

□Lucy's face paled. "But what if he falls after the explosion, that lava is going to spill everywhere inside here. We'll die."

□Rees bowed his head and ran his fingers along the back of his tense neck. "I know. It's a risk we must take."

□He looked at the others. No one seemed convinced.

Brody shouted and pounded his fists against the rock giant's rib cage. "Bob! Let us the fuck out of here now!"

The rock giant laughed, an ear crushing deep hollow sound that echoed throughout the chamber and vibrated under their feet.

Brody looked as if he might be sick.

Rees took a deep breath. "It knows. I thought maybe he couldn't hear us if we spoke out loud, but I was wrong."

"Who knows what?" Brody shouted.

"The evil controlling Bob, it knows we know." Rees dared not add Celia's name to that comment in case there was the slightest chance of keeping that knowledge safe, that he knew she was also not herself. He would continue to protect her until the end.

Brody started to shout but Rees cut him off. "We're wasting time. If we have any chance of surviving we have to kill Bob now, or he'll destroy everyone, and everything. If we don't survive, at least the Earthlings will have a fighting chance."

The room went silent. Everyone was still. The rock giant laughed its horrible laugh again and the chamber swayed. They were flung against the rough walls. Lucy cried out in pain, and Rees shouted at them again to climb up the giants throat. Lucy, Carl, and Cerviias scrambled up the walls and out of sight. But Brody hung back, with Celia next to him. He didn't know why, but he couldn't force them to leave.

It's now or never.

Rees flung his pack off his back and dug inside. He gripped the bag tightly as he was thrown again across the room, as if the rock giant was doing some sort of horrible dance, jumping side to side knowing the contents of its body were being tossed around like rag dolls. He pushed away the pain and kept rummaging inside the bag until he felt it. Hourglass shaped and spongy with long tendrils. He pulled it out. Rees squeezed it a few times, as though he were priming it, until a black goo seeped out. He knew the gift from the pond king would come in handy.

He pumped it a few more times, but the side of his head slammed into the wall. Blood quickly blurred the vision in his right eye. His fingers started to stick together from the black ooze. He pushed himself up, feet unsteady and head swimming. He wobbled towards the magma heart. Inch by inch, using all his might to stay up right. Just as he reached his target, his feet flew out from underneath him.

The sticky residue kept the device tight against his palm.

Rees attempted to stand and was rewarded with shooting pain. He looked down to see his useless twisted leg. He fought the agony coursing through him as he pushed his broken leg back, screaming as he did so that he could use his good leg to crawl once again towards the heart. Each movement jolting him with knives of fire. His vision swam, he wasn't sure he was going to make it to the heart, and just as he was pulled into a pit of misery, he felt something tug on his closed fist.

"Rees let go!" Brody shouted at him.

It took a moment for Rees's brain to catch up. He loosened his grasp, and Brody tugged the malleable black oozing device from his hand. Brody slammed it against the glowing orange heart where it stuck tight.

"What now?" Brody shouted.

Rees tried to scream his reply, and the words caught in his throat. He tried again. "Climb!"

"Shit!" Brody shouted and pulled Rees to his feet. Rees cried out, the extent of his injuries alighting all his pain receptors.

"You can't pull me up a wall Brody." Rees knew this was the end for him. But maybe Celia could be saved. Perhaps whatever was in control of her still had a use for her and would allow her body to climb.

"Take Celia." Rees grabbed tight to Brody's wrist and looked at him intently. "She is not in control of her body. Brody, you must save her." It was perhaps the only time Rees would ever be grateful for Brody's obsession with Celia. He wouldn't let her go without a fight.

Brody nodded, and glanced worriedly one last time at the pulsating device stuck to the heart. "How long?"

"Minutes."

Brody clapped Rees on the back and gave his shoulder a squeeze before yanking Celia by the arm and dragging her to the lumpiest wall with the most footholds and giving her a boost.

Luckily, she complied.

Rees was equal parts relieved and terrified when Celia didn't fight and instead willingly followed Brody up the chamber walls where they could escape through the rock giant's nose. Relieved that she had a chance to survive the impending implosion, yet terrified of what the evil soul controlling her would do with her body once she was on the ground. At least Brody knew the truth. Hopefully he would do whatever was necessary to keep the others safe.

Rees counted. Each second like a nail in his coffin. The black goo stuck to the lava ball started to bubble and glow dark green, like molded moss.

It won't be long now.

Knowing the evil could hear his thoughts, but no longer caring, Rees reached for his father.

"Fridiias? Father? Can you hear me?"

A tear rolled down his cheek as silence engulfed him. Only to have his heart soar moments later when he heard the voice of his father in his head.

"Redreesishual. Son. I am with you."

Rees couldn't stop from crying, the tears flowing out of him bringing some small relief in his final moments.

"Father, I have failed." Rees sent images to his father, summarizing his current situation. Afterwards, when his father knew the extent of his situation, Rees could sense his fathers heartbreak, yet also his desire to comfort his child who was doomed to die.

"You have never failed my son. You have always given your entire self for the benefit of others. That is a life well lived, and never a failure."

Even in his mind, Rees could hear the emotion behind his father's last words.

"Redreesishual, blood of my blood. I am proud of you, my son."

Rees's sobs shook his body. The device had grown to one giant dark green tinted bubble with black strings of ooze dripping down. It had reached peak heat.

He thought then of his Star, and how she would have to live without him. Celia's warmth, her smile, her love. The connection to her had been with him for as long as he could remember. Losing her, would be losing a piece of himself. They were twin flames, never meant to exist without the other. He could only hope that she would find a way to move on, to survive.

He tried to raise his head to look up, only seeing stone but wishing for a chance to see the sky one last time, when the device exploded.

Chapter Twenty-Four

I t, the evil, had complete control of her motor skills. But somewhere, deep, deep, down inside, Celia was still there. Somewhere in her mind she clung to consciousness. It laughed at her efforts as though it was futile to try and stick around. Its vile laugh echoed all around her but no one else could hear.

Its foul happiness sickened her.

The evil's anticipation grew as they got closer and closer to the Earth territory, lighting up every nerve ending in Celia's body. She hated the sensation within herself that was not her own. The thought of anyone, or anything, exhibiting excited anticipation to destroy an entire population made Celia feel horrible sickly things she didn't have words for. The evil laughed at her. It spoke to her.

"I'm going to make a chain from their guts and string them from the trees."

The nauseous ball in her gut rolled.

"I'll slit their throats and drain the blood onto their babies for them to choke on."

A tear rolled down her cheek, and her teeth chattered.

"I'll go slow, one by one until all you see is red."

Bile burned her throat.

She didn't know if she'd have the strength to continue life if she was forced to watch her own hands kill everyone she loved. Her mother, her father, her friends. The thought made her want to give up. To turn off her mind and let the evil take over every last granule of herself that was still hanging on. If she gave up the fight, maybe she wouldn't have to see the destruction about to take place. It would be so much easier to give in. To lose.

Suddenly, the ground beneath her feet shook. It was a numb sensation, still being removed from her body, but strong enough to get her full attention. Her body swung around to see the rock giant exploding. Her eyes scanned the surrounding ground, taking inventory of her friends, but truly only searching for one.

Rees.

Where was he?

When she saw Lucy sink to her knees, she knew. Rees was still inside.

She shrieked an animalistic unnatural sound, and felt a tingle in her fingertips. Screaming at the top of her lungs she shrugged Brody off her arm and lunged towards the fire. Every step brought her closer to herself. She was taking back control and expelling the evil little by little as her desire to reach Rees increased. Her single-minded goal to reach the man that she loved drowned everything else out.

Feeling came back. Slow at first, and then fast like a river.

Not Rees.

Her feet pounded the ground and suddenly her breathing was no longer muffled. The evil sank somewhere far within her and yowled as though it had fallen into a deep well inside her gut, and then, it was gone. Celia had her body, mind, and soul back. She was her own self again. But there was no time to celebrate as she approached the towering inferno.

The rock giant was now a huge mound of boulder and molten lava that was spreading out fast and hot and lighting everything green on fire. She scoured the area searching for any sign of life, desperate to find him.

He had to have gotten out before the explosion.

She screamed out. "Rees!"

I can't lose him.

Dread filled her veins as her blood pulsed cold through her body as her teeth chattered while she ran. There was no losing him. There was no her without him. From the moment their eyes met she felt a connection profound in her soul as if he had always been there with her. Losing him was just as bad as losing herself.

She screamed again and it came out strangled and desperate. "Rees! Answer me!"

Ahead of her lay the ruins of the rock giant, its lava blood spilled out like a river. As she got closer the heat became so thick and strong it was hard to breathe. She coughed on the hotness of it. She scanned the surroundings for any sign of Rees, growing more fraught by the second.

Finally, in the distance she saw him, laying on the ground on the other side of a molten lava river. She looked to either side, searching for a way around but finding none. The lava had spread too far creating a ravine between them.

A feeling grew inside her. Similar to the despair she felt months ago when she ran from the sanctuary, and when she watched the rabbit turn blue and die. Only now, it was amplified by thousands. It filled her so much she thought she would drown on it, and just when she thought she might suffocate, something spilled out of her.

Only it wasn't emotion.

It was tangible.

A solid black tar that oozed from her pores, thick and crackling like electricity on fire.

The electric ooze continued to spill from her. Celia's breathing came out fast and scared.

What is happening to me?

She stood frozen, full of terror and heartbreak. She couldn't process what was happening to her when her heart still ached for Rees. Her tear-filled eyes flashed to his body across the way.

If she was dying, she wanted to die beside him.

She took a step forward. And the ooze followed. She reached a hand forward and the ooze slithered forward.

I can control it.

She brought her hands flat together. Palm against palm and aimed towards the lava river. The ooze continued to pour out of her, spilling down her eyes, nose, and every surface of her body until she no longer had to move her feet because the ooze moved her. It formed a bridge over the lava and she rode the ooze straight across, slowly and deliberately towards Rees.

She extended an arm to wrap herself around Rees when a voice loud and urgent forced itself upon her, stopping her mid motion.

"Stop. Your touch will kill him!" The masculine voice shouted in her head.

She pulled her arm back and her heart raced.

Does that mean he's alive? She glanced at Rees and stared, desperately searching for the rise and fall of his chest. Seeing every cut, gash, and bruise across his battered body. His eyes remained closed, but there was a slight movement behind the lids, as if he were simply dreaming.

He's alive.

Relief so profound she didn't have words to express came over her. Her heart thumped against her chest as she embraced the wave of gratitude. Her focus switched to the faintly familiar voice. It wasn't the evil, but someone else. The memory was there, just out of reach.

"Who is this?" She asked.

"Fridiias, father of Redreesishual."

For reasons she didn't understand, an immense calm wafted over Celia like a blanket. The idea that she was no longer alone in the fight for Rees's life. That help was just around the corner. The realization reset her and extinguished the black ooze. It left behind only a faint blue sparking until that too dissipated.

Her hands started to shake and her teeth chattered again, just like massive amounts of adrenaline leaving her body. "Do you know what this is? What's happening to me?" She asked Fridiias.

"I do. Before it was only a theory, but I believe that theory to be confirmed after what I just witnessed."

"Well..." She said, anxious for more of an explanation.

The voice paused before continuing, and just when she thought she might scream, Fridiias spoke to her again. "Long ago, when my son's soul found yours, I watched you just as he did. I had to know if you were a threat to my child. I observed your ability to absorb the poison on Earth as an infant. But where did that poison go? The poison was caused by all the bad, evil, and hateful things on your home planet and transformed.

Essentially, the poison began as energy, as all things do. But energy cannot be destroyed. So I guessed that it was simply being stored within you. You are a vessel. You take energy, but you also give energy. Unfortunately, your stored energy is lethal. Anything you disperse contains years of malevolent energy.

Simply put, you are, or rather your ooze is, radioactive."

Again, the thought of the rabbit flashed in her mind. The poison had built up too much and wanted to spill out of her. She was more dangerous than any body snatching entity.

"What do I do?" She pleaded.

"The energy will come out one way or another. All you can hope for is to send it in the right direction. And that direction must be far away from my son." He said with determination and a hint of threat in his voice.

The last thing she wanted to do was hurt Rees. He must know that, right? She truly didn't want to hurt anybody, and she was struggling to accept this deep dark thing that had been catching a ride in her body for so many years. Wasn't an evil soul possession enough? She got rid of that, and now she had to deal with a new form of evil?

It wasn't fair, it wasn't right.

"Fortify your mind girl! Do you want that soul to take you back? It preys on the weak. Waits until the mind is vulnerable, then hops right on in." Fridiias shouted.

She thought of everyone that would be at risk because of her, or at least her body's mercy if she lost herself again. She couldn't let that happen. Celia took a deep breath and told herself to handle one problem at a time. Now that she was no longer possessed, at least for the time being, she needed to focus on Rees. The toxicity would have to wait.

"He needs a doctor. Where are you? Will you help me?" Celia asked.

"I want nothing more than to save my son. But I cannot. I am still imprisoned and it is taking all my willpower to communicate with you across the distance without detection. I have merely a few moments left until I must leave you. This world is counting on you, daughter of the savior. You must find a way. You must save him. I've done all I can. It's up to you now. I am counting on you."

She felt rather than heard his presence leave.

A wave of cold washed over her. Celia felt more alone now than ever before. She glanced down to Rees's broken body, all the cuts, bumps, and bruises, and his chest barely rising. There wasn't time to leave him here in search of help.

Especially outside of the Sanctuary border. She didn't know the natural predators of this stretch of wild land. What if she left him only to be attacked as soon as she was gone.

She thought back to years before when her father subjected her to hours of first aid lessons in anticipation of her first time babysitting a younger child. One of those lessons was what to do in case of a fire, and the fireman carry he taught her. Only Rees was no child, she wouldn't simply be able to toss him over her shoulder.

She made sure that all the toxicity was safely stored back in her body so that she wouldn't hurt him when she touched him. Then she laid down next to him, then pulled his left leg over the top of her left leg. Then she used his body weight to roll them both to their sides. Celia then pulled his left arm across her shoulders and rolled further, as though he was giving her a hug from behind, his front on her back. From this position, it was not easy, but possible to rise to her knees and then to a half stand with Rees on her back.

She struggled under the weight of him, but took slow small steps forward. Until her body burned and her legs shook. One step at a time, until she got used to the weight and could take slightly bigger and faster steps. They were so close to the Sanctuary border when the giant had exploded. She had less than a mile to walk. And just as she reached the top of a grassy hill, she could see the border. Help was close.

It took her a moment to make sense of the scene before her as a harsh wind blew against her sweaty brow. There seemed to be a line or group of people next to the edge of the border. It looked frantic. But the guards of Meraiis were steadfast on their side of the border, watching at the ready, as the people of Earth fought each other.

Celia's heart sank. They were too late. They made it back in time before the Earthlings attacked the people of Meraiis, but not soon enough to stop the evil souls from taking over some of the members of the Sanctuary. Brother fought brother, and sister fought sister. It seemed as though it was impossible to tell who was possessed and who was not. But the longer she watched, the more she could see. Some of the people had a crazed look about them. All black eyes and snarling faces.

She pulled her gaze away from her people and took a few more steps until finally one of the Meraiias guards saw her approaching. They drew their sword and telepathically ordered her to stop.

"This man needs help." She shouted out loud with a desperate cry in her voice before collapsing to the ground, and carefully rolling Rees off her and onto his back.

"You are on the wrong side of your border, human. What is the meaning of all this?" They gestured to the Earthlings fighting each other. "Some kind of distraction? One minute your people are accusing us of kidnapping some child, and the next they are tearing each other to pieces. Tell me what you know!"

Celia realized they didn't know about evil soul possession. The Meraiis penchant for staying out of all things, must have kept them out of the war all those years ago. Their determination to not intervene had built an ignorance within their race. They didn't even know about a war that took place on their own planet. Or at the very least this generation was not taught the history of it. Perhaps she'd be able to use their ignorance to her benefit.

"Not until you help him." She replied with fire in her eyes and nodded to Rees.

The guard hesitated, staring at her reluctantly as if weighing their options. Finally, they pulled open a cross-body bag. From within they took out a yellow glowing orb. They kneeled next to Rees and placed the orb gently on his forehead while whispering something in the Meraiis language.

"It is done. If he can be healed, he will be healed." They took a deep breath and fixed her with a death stare. "Now speak, tell me what you know."

It was Celia's turn to hesitate. She knew there were traitors within the Meraiis government, including some of their own guards. But this particular guard didn't seem to recognize her, or realize she was the 'kidnapped child'. So she guessed they weren't aware of the subterfuge within their own kind.

She took a deep breath. She stared one last time at her people destroying each other. Nails clawing flesh, fists breaking eye sockets, and gargled cries. So much blood. Celia then looked at Rees and his broken body that may or may not heal. She decided to protect him as best she could by not telling the guard about the plot to take The Origin from Rees, nor informing the guard of who Rees is. All the blood and dirt hid most of his features.

But she told them everything else instead. How the evil souls were possessing her people. How the Cinis dust was the only thing that could kill the evil souls and evaporate it back to nothingness.

"So do you understand?" She asked. "We must find my friends. They must have been possessed before they could accomplish their task. They have the Cinis bulbs, we must bury the bulbs so the plants can grow and spread their pollen. It's the only hope my people have to fight this wicked siege. Please, help me."

The guard had a torn look upon his face. "It is our orders to not intervene unless the treaty is broken. As of yet, your people have not trespassed."

A wave of defeat washed over Celia, until she realized. "What about me? I have passed across the border, therefore the treaty has been broken. My kind can spill upon your land at any moment, you must defend your territory."

She could see the realization in the guards eyes. They understood the loophole she had found. They smiled. "You are correct, Earthling. We must defend our land. We will help you find your friends and plant the Cinis seeds."

Celia's relief was so fierce she nearly cried on the spot. She held herself together though, and relayed to the guards what her friends looked like. One of them had to have the seeds in their bag as she knew Rees wouldn't have sent her friends ahead without the seeds, and her own bag was missing. Brody, or one of the others had to have it.

Celia and the Meraiis guards rushed forward. Mud sprayed the ground as she ran. The moment her foot crossed the border she was bombarded with energy so intense she nearly crumbled. All the nasty, vicious, devilish things happening had built up such an intense cloud of energy that it was immediately sucked into Celia's body the second she passed the invisible shield separating the two lands.

Screams echoed in her mind. Her vision swam and she squeezed her eyes shut. Images of brutality flooded the darkness behind her lids. The pain of others invaded her body. There was no stopping the inundation. She fell to the ground, curled up into a ball, and screamed out, yet the screams of others were so intense she could no longer hear herself.

A boiling pot of fear, agony, and despair built within herself until it could no longer be contained. The black tar-like substance crackling with white electric sparks and blue flames shot out from her body in all directions like a bomb, decimating everything and everyone in its wake.

The fire burned hot within her. Images of every horrible life experience she had ever absorbed from anyone besieged her. Hundreds of lifetime's worth of moments. The burning emotional turmoil was so all-consuming she imagined it spread not just all across this planet, but that it must spread to every corner of the universe.

She had always imagined the universe dying slowly, like a tree. It roots slowly bit by bit, diseased, and starved until it eventually would succumb to its ailments and slowly fall back unto the ground. But here it was, death. Fast, unforgiving, torturous, and all by her hand.

Chapter Twenty-Five

□The ground beneath him shook as Rees slowly opened his eyes. Every inch of his body ached, his muscles and joints from his head all the way down to his toes. He carefully rose to a seated position. Rees patted his body down searching for fractures, cuts, or any other injury. Finding nothing but soreness was something he couldn't explain, until he felt the orb stuck to his forehead. He peeled it off and saw the healing orb, which starts out yellow and glowing, but was now a pale cream color and dull. Whatever injuries he sustained, had completely used up every ounce of healing power the orb could provide.

□He gingerly stood and stared all around him, squinting from the sun and seeing nothing until he looked up. The grassy knoll in front of him blocked his direct line of sight, but above it was a massive cloud of energy strings all rolled into a tangled giant ball writhing like a nest of snakes.

Celia.

Rees knew it was his woman. The tangle of angry strands told him she was struggling, battling against an onslaught of evil. He pushed his pain down and ran towards the mass.

As he crested the hill he spotted her instantly. Twitching on the ground, hands clapped to her ears as though trying to block out an incredible noise. All around her lay unconscious bodies. Meraiin and humans alike, all a sea of paralyzed fear. He hurried to her side and collapsed to his knees.

Cautiously, he leaned over her, searching for a way to help. Rees tried to pull Celia's hands away from her ears to bring them into his own, but they were stiff and solidly stuck to her ears attempting to block out whatever she was hearing. He couldn't detect anything that would be causing her such torment. A deep, unexplainable buzz did surround them. As if thousands of bees were trapped underground, but it was not nearly loud enough to cause discomfort, let alone whatever his love was feeling.

"Celia!" He shouted. "Open your eyes! Please, my Star, open your eyes!"

He received no response. Celia continued to be stiff and quivering, frozen on the ground. It agonized him to see her this way and not be able to help her. Rees lay his head on her chest and begged through his weeping for her to come back to him. He ran his fingers through her dark curls and longed to see the bright gray of her beautiful eyes. He felt the softness of her cheek and saw the rose in her lips and yearned to taste them one last time, but couldn't bear to put his lips to hers when she was clearly so trapped within her own mind. He needed her in a way that transcends physicality. Rees could not live without her essence of self, her mind.

 Her shaking suddenly stopped and Rees lifted his head to stare at her hoping she was coming out of her trance. But her hands slapped flat to the ground, her body stiff as a board against the dirt. And when her eyes opened, he did not see her spark of life, but swirling clouds of black. Her jaw fell open in a silent scream.

 "Celia!" Rees shouted. "Someone! Anyone! Please help her!" He cried out.

 "Son. Calm yourself."

 "Father?"

 "You cannot help her if you fall into despair."

 "What shall I do, father? Please, help me. I cannot lose her."

 "You are the most powerful among us, even more so than the evil that keeps hold over her... You have the Origin. Son, you must look inside yourself, access it. All living things across the entirety of the universe are connected in one way or another, you know this, you see this all around you. The answer is somewhere within that connectivity. You must simply find it."

 "That's too much father. There's too much to access. I can't make sense of it all. Her spark is the only thing that has ever called to me with such clarity."

 "Then that is your answer, you must find her spark. You have only ever listened, son, now you must speak. Speak so that she may find her voice again. Speak so that you may find her again. Energy, soul, never dies. It exists in infinity. You must simply find her specific frequency. Which should be easy... as she is a part of you, and you are of her. Soulmates. You can do this son. Start with the soil beneath you, a firm foundation to extend your search."

◻Having the Origin inside him was like having a second skin. One that he hadn't worn since Celia's soul had called to him all those years ago. He had only ever gotten lost in all the noise whenever he tried to access the limitlessness of the universe. Getting lost in all that knowledge terrified Rees. But he looked again at his Star, and it was clear he was losing her. He couldn't let that happen. He had to try everything in his power to save her.

◻Rees took three deep breaths, letting each out slowly, and then placed his palms against the ground. He closed his eyes and opened his heart. The ground was cool to the touch. Beneath that, ants scurried, and beneath that roots grew. He followed those roots to their hosts, and followed those hosts to their link in the chain of interconnected life until he no longer saw the deer, birds, or humans, but instead saw their energy. The frequencies that connected all things. They hummed against his brain, each like their own unique song, and those songs echoed to the cosmos. The brightness of space. The color of the stars against the blackness of space.

The stars like rain, shining and falling into infinity.

He followed the stars to where he first linked with Celia's song. And what he found there filled him with wonder, happiness, and hope. They would need to know, all of the humans, what he had found there, but first he followed the echo of her song. He traveled back towards Meraiis, and as he approached, her frequency grew stronger and stronger, until at last he had found her.

There she lay, flickering in the darkness, a light fighting to not be extinguished. He went to her, and found himself being blocked by the electric sparks of evil. Rees fought back. Pushing and tearing his way through the sparks. But they simply regrew, refusing to let him through. So he searched further, past the sparks, to see where they could not reach. There, he found his answer. Like trees soaking up carbon dioxide to produce oxygen, the paliios, what Earthlings would call butterflies, absorbed the evil and weaved it into a web of goodness. He sought out the paliios, and called to them. He presented them with his struggle and inquired if any of them would be willing to give themselves to her.

Rees pulled himself out of the Origin, out of the interconnectedness of the universe, and back into his body. He opened his eyes, placed his hand next to Celia's and waited. His heart beating against his ribs with anticipation, and then filled with warmth when he saw them. The cloud of soaring color. The paliios flying as one in their direction. A beautiful rainbow of fluttering wings refracting flashes of sunlight. They gently landed one by one upon Celia's body, attaching themselves there until she was covered in a blanket of beauty.

Their wings opened and closed, pulsing and breathing as one against her body. Slowly, the clouds cleared from her eyes. Color returned to her face. Warmth returned to her body. Her hands closed and her head turned. Then, there she was, staring at him with a smile upon her lips, as if seeing him through the film of a dream.

"Rees."

The sound of his voice from her tongue was a lyric he never wanted to lose.

"My Star." He said with all the joy from his soul.

He wrapped his arms around her and pulled her to him.

She tucked her head under his chin and nuzzled his chest. "I thought I lost you."

"You almost did my Star. But I found you. I'll always find you." The feel of her pulse against his skin stoked the fire burning within him. He was home. She was his home.

Rees looked out at the sea of unconscious people. A wave of paliios had blanketed them, and one by one the people awakened.

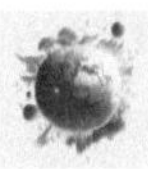

Hours later, they had finally planted the last of the cinis bulbs. They shot out of the ground as fully grown plants within minutes. The sanctuary was safe once again.

"Well, I don't know about you, but I'd like to never be possessed ever again for as long as I live. Just feed me to the sharks if I ever have to do that shit again." Carl said with exasperation in his voice.

"Woah, Carl, coming out with the big words." Lucy joked as she nudged his shoulder.

They all knew Carl was the most reserved of the group and rarely swore.

"And how exactly are we supposed to prevent this from happening again if we don't even know how it happened in the first place?" Brody grunted. He still seemed a but bitter that Rees was the one to have saved the day.

Celia rolled her eyes at his attitude, but he did have a point. "You're not wrong, Brody."

"Well, duh, of course I'm not wrong, Celia." He gave her a smile and winked.

Their old banter seemed to be returning, much to Rees's disappointment, but to Celia's delight. She did miss her old friend. But she knew, and Rees knew, that what her and Rees shared was far greater than any friendship between her and Brody.

One of the paliios fluttered away and another one returned in its place. Unlike the others, Celia would have the constant company of the butterflies. Her ability to absorb evil needed an outlet. Never again could she allow such toxicity to build within her, putting everyone and everything she loved at risk, now that she knew she did not eliminate negativity, she simply stored it.

Rees, who somehow seemed even more enlightened, appeared to have the answers to everything. "We cannot prevent evil from happening. Years ago, during the war that accompanied your arrival."

"That's a polite way to say the war that humans brought with them and started against the Aniimarus." Celia spoke quietly.

Rees gave her a knowing look of acknowledgement before continuing. "During that war, the General was not eliminated, only injured. He and the remaining soldiers went into a state of hibernation, absorbing as much bad energy as they could, believing that was the only way to grow in power, and they waited until they were strong enough to inhabit more than just the animals and the Aniimarus. It was the General that did this."

"My mother isn't going to like this." Celia said.

"She needn't worry." Rees replied. "The paliios have transformed him to good, it is most likely that he, and his soldiers, have finally found peace and moved on." He hesitated. "But there will always be different forms of evil. The universe requires balance, and good cannot exist without evil. But we can protect ourselves, and put as much good into the world as we can."

Carl, Lucy, and Brody had a touch of uncertainty in their eyes, but none of them said anything.

Celia sighed. "Well, on that note. I promised my mom and dad a complete debrief as soon as we were done here, so I better go check in with them. I'm sure they have a lot of questions."

Rees stood and brushed the dirt from his hands. She noticed how beautifully his violet eyes glowed in the sun, and his black skin practically shimmered against the warmth. "I'll go with you."

Celia patted his arm. "I think I should go alone."

Rees pulled her close. Her skin tingled as he swept curls off her shoulders. "I respect your wishes, my Star." He said. "But there are things I have not shared, and we must discuss them all together."

She pulled away. "What things? What aren't you telling me?"

He tugged her back to him, smiled, and whispered to her ears. "Don't worry, my Star. It's good. You'll like the news, I promise."

Her skin tingled again and her heart raced as his lips brushed her neck as he pulled away.

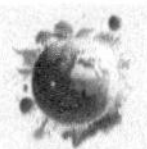

The talk with Celia's parents went even better than he expected, and he was excited for the journey ahead. The only left to do was to approach the council and demand to be heard. His father must be released, and his claim to the Origin must be respected. He no longer harbored fear now that he had fully embraced who he was and his place in this world. Accessing the Origin had given him such a great sense of self and purpose, he no longer concerned himself with the politics of Meraiis. He and his birth father, Fridiias, the last holder of the Origin, were the only ones still alive who knew the truth of who his people were. Their complete history and how they had arrived at this place of avoidance, denial, and cruelty.

He approached the capital with an army at his back. Made up of his Aniimarus family, thousands of the evolved deer, his new human friends, and Celia by his side.

The Meraiis citizens all gasped in disbelief at his approach. Staring at him, wild eyed, and not understanding how he could be so bold as to walk through the front gates so unbothered. As they got closer to the capitol, a much smaller army blocked their path, with Dairea and Tiimas at the front.

Dairea screeched at the capitol guards. "Arrest them, now!"

The capitol guards took in the full strength in numbers of the army standing behind Rees, and waivered. They looked at each other with uncertainty and fear in their eyes. It was obvious they did not have the resolve to follow orders when they were so clearly outnumbered.

Tiimas shouted. "What is the matter with you? Did you not hear her? Arrest them!"

Rees smiled. "Do not worry my neighbors, for we are all one on this planet. There is no need for a divide."

The guards lowered their swords and cleared them a path. Rees nodded to Dairea and Tiimas as they passed. Dairea stared with her mouth agape and fury in her eyes. Tiimas stomped a foot and shouted. "This is outrageous!" His voice trailed off as Rees and the others continued on their way.

As they entered the great hive and made their way to the throne room, no one else attempted to stop them.

When they arrived, Rees took his place at the center, and his friends and family took their seats in the front. The deer waited outside. It didn't take long for the stadium-like palace to fill up. Word traveled fast within the hive.

When the space was full, Rees addressed the masses. "Welcome." His voice echoed in the Meraiis language and he held his arms open wide as he looked around the chambers. When he had their attention, he continued. "As many of you must have surmised, there have been developments within our community. The first and most important of those developments is that I have accepted my claim to the Origin."

There came a murmuring from the crowd, like a low buzz that traveled back and forth across the chambers.

Rees held a hand up. "I order the release of my father, Fridiias, immediately. Dairea and Tiimas will be held for treason until the council can agree upon a sound punishment."

A commotion came from the outer ring of the hive. Tiimas had tried to make a run for it, and Dairea was sobbing on the floor. But the guards did not hesitate to switch sides and follow Rees's orders once they felt the full effect of the power radiating out of him.

When the chambers settled, Rees continued. The other development is that we as a civilization will no longer turn a blind eye to those in need that we are able to help."

A roar of dissent rose from the masses.

"SILENCE!" Rees shouted, blazing with the power of aeons of years of knowledge that boiled within him. The energy was palpable.

Quiet descended immediately, and he once again had the full attention of the court.

Rees spoke. "This decision is not up for debate. However, I will force no one to help in our quest to assist others. It will be volunteer based exclusively. I will never force another soul to ever do anything against their wishes. We are a race of freedom. Freedom that was hard earned long, long ago."

He paused momentarily when he saw his birth father escorted into the hive. He looked older, more tired, but alive and in one piece. A smile crinkled the corner of his eyes, a proud father seeing his son take his rightful place in the world.

Rees felt tears of happiness build within himself. He embraced the warm energy his father sent across the room before he again addressed the Meraiin people.

"Long, long, long ago, we were once a connected hive mind, until one day, the Origin, with its spark of self-awareness, woke one of our own. They were called Stathos One. Stathos One, unknowingly, awoke more and more of our kind. Giving way to independent thought... to freedom. Eventually a group of us broke off on our own to explore the universe.

Planet after planet was studied, as we searched for a place to call home, until finally we found a planet called Earth. The people of Earth however, were not all welcoming to our kind. Thousands of years passed as we battled for a place to call our own on Earth's surface. Until... Stathos One, fell in love with a human.

The battles between humans and aliens ended.

Stathos One started a new family and instead of passing the Origin to his offspring, Stathos One passed the Origin to another of his kind who, with others, decided to move on from Earth to find a new home. This new group traveled the universe once again, until they found Meraiis. We made Meraiis our new home, and vowed to never again intervene in the dealings of others, for fear of repeating the battles that happened on Earth."

Rees paused to give the citizens time to process everything he had said.

Then he continued. "But that was then. And now, we have a chance to help others. Cries travel to us from all across the universe, and we have the knowledge and the power to help many of them. We did not intervene, and that was the right choice then. But time has brought changes to all things, and we must change with them. We must not continue to ignore the cries of the desperate when we can put good back into the cosmos."

He slowly looked around the hive and saw many mixed emotions. Some agreed and some did not. "So... to those willing to help, I call upon you to come with me. I will be leading the first voyage of rescue, and hopefully you will all see the good that we can do."

Dozens of Meraiin made their way down to the front, and kneeled before him. Rees, filled with gratitude, focused on delivering his last decree.

"And finally, we will allow the people of the Sanctuary, who crash landed here so many years ago, the freedom to explore the planet as our equals."

A roar of contempt spread throughout the chamber. Many words of poison and evil flared within the shouts.

Rees's adopted father, the Aniimarus leader, Oisin, calmly made his way to the center of the space and stood stoically in front of his son. His massive frame, much larger than any of the Meraiin, quieted the chambers.

Oisin spoke telepathically to them all. "If anyone has a right to be outraged, it is the Aniimarus." He fixed them all with a stare of fire for when the Meraiin refused to help the Aniimarus all those years ago. "But the Earthlings have grown in wisdom, and that wisdom is rewarded with freedom. We do not have to fear their poison. Our planet is uniquely designed to process their ailment. I will not deny that it will come with changes, but nature is an ever-evolving thing, and we must accept this change for the greater good. We cannot contain such a great force as that of humanity, for then it will only fester into a great wound on our world."

The impact of his words brought silence to the chamber.

Rees walked to Oisin and embraced him with pride in his eyes.

His adopted mother, Aoife and his brothers, Padraig, and Darragh all joined in and they held each other in a familial group hug. His joy and gratitude for all the good things that had come his way, overwhelmed him.

He searched for his anchor, Celia. She felt him searching for her, and soon after, felt her hand slip into his. The Aniimarus broke free, all smiles with pointed teeth.

Rees addressed the hive one last time. "When such a time comes that I wish to retire from my aid of the universe. I will pass the Origin, not to my offspring, but to the next leader of search and rescue. The Origin from this day forward, will only be given to those of pure heart, who wish to use its knowledge to help others, not to control the masses.

Until we meet again, thank you for your time."

Rees bowed to the crowd.

Despite some lingering disgruntlement from the hive, they dispersed without further incident and Rees was left with contentment beside his family, friends, and his Star.

Epilogue

Excitement bubbled all the way down to her toes as Celia danced in anticipation of arrival. Herself, Rees, Brody, Lucy, Carl, and about a dozen others, both human and Meraiin alike, including her parents, were aboard the mothership traveling across the universe, on their way to a pit stop before their first official rescue mission.

"Can you believe it mom?" Celia exclaimed with delight.

Téa shook her head. "No. Actually. Really… I can't believe it." She turned around. "Rees, tell me one last time, what was it that you saw during your search in the Origin for Celia?"

Rees smiled and grasped his soon to be mother-in-law's hands. "I saw Earth. The meteor that hit the planet all those years ago did indeed cause significant damage. But the planet was not unlivable. In sections of the Earth, air was still breathable, birds, bees, plants, and others all remained. Life on Earth is thriving."

Téa looked at him with tears in her eyes and a smile on her face. She tried to speak, but the words were stuck in her throat. She gulped and tried again. "And the other thing?" She said hesitantly. "Tell me again, one last time." She squeezed his hands.

Rees leaned in closer, speaking softly. "The bullet that took Annabelle, your sister, hit her chest, but no significant organs. When you sealed her with all the Earth-like things, what you thought was her final resting place, was actually her shelter. The egg-like grave you gave her overlooking the waterfall, actually protected her from the impact of the meteor. The egg fell down the waterfall and traveled along the river to a safe zone, and... it gave her body time to use its Connex healing powers. Slowly, her body pushed the bullet out and healed itself. When you saw and communicated with her spirit, you both didn't know it, but she was not dead, merely in a suspended state, like a coma. And when you could no longer find her spirit to talk to, it was not because she had crossed over, but because her spirit had returned to her fully healed body."

Téa grinned ear to ear and whispered. "My sister is alive?"

"Yes." Rees said. "And thriving. She is the leader of a community of survivors. They have built a new home, a better home, a fresh start."

Téa turned back around to smile at her daughter, then stood and went into the arms of her husband. "Zephyr, can you believe it? She's alive."

"Yes my Star, I believe it. You both deserve this. The universe has given you a gift." He squeezed her tighter and kissed the top of her head.

Celia was so happy to see again the love her parents shared. It had been so long, and it reminded her to never take Rees for granted. She lifted her hand, and the butterflies fluttered away to her shoulder, and there from beneath them shone the brilliant blue gemstone Rees had placed on her finger only days before. Like the butterflies, it was a welcome, and permanent accessory that brought immeasurable euphoria to her soul.

The mothership touched down to Earth only a few miles away from Annabelle's settlement. The moment the ship's doors opened, Téa sprinted down the field. Her legs pumped, and heart raced, pushing forward and desperate to see the truth with her own eyes. As she crested a hill, Téa saw the settlement below.

She had to force herself to slow down or she would end up rolling down the hill uncontrollably. Step by careful step brought her closer and closer to her heart, her soulmate. The people of the settlement stared at her in shock. They probably hadn't seen a new person in a long time.

"Annabelle!" Téa shouted out. Calling her name again and again. Shouting her name and running through the village.

Until finally, she saw her in the distance.

Annabelle.

Hands deep in the soil, in her natural element, helping things to grow. Téa slowed to a walk, hands shaking, and happy tears streaming down her face. Her breathing ragged and legs weak, walking, closer and closer, until Annabelle paused, as if she felt her before she saw her. Annabelle lifted her head, and their eyes locked.

Sister.

Acknowledgements

I started my professional writing journey late in 2022, and since that time I've had the great privilege of meeting and virtually connecting with amazingly wonderful people in the writing and publishing world.

I could not have learned, grown, and improved my craft without my critique partners; Julia Sung, Liahona West, Amanda Stuntz, and Kari Robinson. I will forever cherish their encouragement and support.

There have been many alpha and beta readers along the way, too many to name, but please know, if you were an early reader for me, I truly appreciated and listened to every bit of feedback I was ever offered.

Lilian Zenzi, the first fellow writer that I got to meet in person, and someone who is a force of positivity. Marisa E. Cardin who hosted the first author event I ever attended, I look forward to what's still to come!

Jennifer Givhan, one of my favorite authors, and who despite her success in this world still took the time to write one of my very first official blurbs for the back cover of Stars Like Acid, and has since continued to be a beacon of light.

All of the social media influencers who have taken the time to read, review, or share about the books, I am tremendously grateful to you all. If you're not following, The Writers Community Promo Page, Mae and the Indie Speak Easy, Rozanne Visagie, or Carlys Growing TBR, then you definitely should.

Jolee, owner of the Satisfiction book box, who took a chance on me and Stars Like Acid. I am eternally grateful to you and your vision to highlight BIPOC authors.

The indie bookstores that stocked my books on their shelves. White River Books in Carbondale CO, Quail Ridge Books in Raleigh NC, Black Dahlia tattoo studio in Prescott Valley AZ, and especially Salient Books where they are "All Indie all the Time", please check them out!

The Barnes and Noble locations in Lakewood/Golden Colorado and Boulder Colorado who hosted my first book signings in an actual book store. Thank you to the management and staff there, you're amazing!

My local library in Meeker Colorado who has stocked all my books and hosted all of my book release parties. Thank you Kristina. Libraries are invaluable, please use them!

My husband, Jason, who makes the time to do all my graphic design and cover art. And who has never told me I can't do something I want to do, and who has always supported me in everything I have set my mind to. An amazing father to our three boys, I love you.

To my mom for being my biggest cheerleader.

To all the readers... you have brought me out of the darkness. You keep my heart happy, and motivate me to keep going even when it's hard. You'll never know how much it means to me that you have taken the time to read my stories. Thank you!

And finally to my sister Chelsea, for always having my back, you complete me.

About the Author

Marissa Lupe, Latina/Indigenous (she/her) of mixed
heritage, has always found her safe place in the world of

stories. Now, she's creating her own worlds in the scope of speculative fiction and hopes to provide the same joy to her readers.

Her first published series includes three books plus a prequel; Stars Like Acid, Stars Like Fire, Stars Like Rain, and The Bone Inventory. Her first novel, Stars Like Acid, was included in the Satisfiction book box in late 2024, and was mentioned as a book to read by Winter Is Coming dot Net. Her third novel, The Bone Inventory, was nominated as 'Jaw Dropper', 'Gives Me Goosebumps', 'Fearless Female Storyteller', and 'Anti Hero I Cheered For' through the Indieverse Awards.

Marissa has been selected as a speaker at the, A Million Lives book festival 2025, and was featured in Voyage Denver Magazine December of 2024. She has book outlines for over a dozen novels and looks forward to all the stories that are to come.

Beyond writing, Marissa enjoys anything artsy and creative, like making jewelry, painting, photography, and collecting crystals. She currently lives in the Rocky Mountains of western Colorado with her family, connecting with the soul of the Earth through the appreciation of nature.

www.ingramcontent.com/pod-product-compliance
Lightning Source LLC
Chambersburg PA
CBHW020752310726
48969CB00002B/497